OMEGA:

THE LAST DAYS OF THE WORLD

BY

CAMILLE FLAMMARION

WITH ILLUSTRATIONS BY
JEAN PAUL LAURENS, SAUNIER, MÉAULLE, VOGEL, ROCHEGROSSE, GERADIN,
CHOVIN, TOUSSAINT, GUILLONNET, SCHWABE, AND OTHERS

INTRODUCTION TO THE BISON BOOKS EDITION BY
ROBERT SILVERBERG

UNIVERSITY OF NEBRASKA PRESS
LINCOLN AND LONDON

Introduction © 1999 by the University of Nebraska Press
All rights reserved
Manufactured in the United States of America

⊗

First Bison Books printing: 1999
Most recent printing indicated by the last digit below:
10   9   8   7   6   5   4   3   2   1

Library of Congress Cataloging-in-Publication Data
Flammarion, Camille, 1842–1925.
[Fin du monde. English]
Omega: the last days of the world / by Camille Flammarion;
introduction to the Bison Books edition by Robert Silverberg.
p.   cm.
ISBN 0-8032-6898-X (pbk.: alk. paper)
I. Title.
PQ2244.F9F513   1999
843'.8—dc21
98-51566   CIP

Reprinted from the original 1894 edition by The Cosmopolitan
Publishing Company, New York. This Bison Books edition follows
the original in beginning chapter 1 on arabic page 7; no material
has been omitted.

INTRODUCTION

ROBERT SILVERBERG

Camille Flammarion was one of the most profoundly imaginative of the nineteenth-century science-fiction pioneers, and his extraordinary apocalyptic novel, *Omega: The Last Days of the World*, first published in 1893 in French, was a famous work in its time. It was translated into eleven languages and exercised a powerful influence on the thinking of a great many visionary novelists, including Jules Verne and H.G. Wells, during the years immediately following its publication. Yet it has somehow slipped into almost total neglect since then, and in the English-speaking world it is virtually unknown. The only English translation, published in 1894 by the Cosmopolitan Publishing Company of New York and since then reprinted only once, has long been a nearly unobtainable rarity.

Flammarion (1842–1925) was a practicing astronomer for whom writing was a secondary profession. He maintained a private observatory at Juvissy, just south of Paris, where he devoted himself to the study of the movements of the planets and to the observation of unusual stellar phenomena—most notably Nova Persei of 1903, the first nova that had been seen since the great supernova of 1604 and the subject of a memorable study by Johannes Kepler. Flammarion detected a rapidly expanding ring of luminous gases surrounding Nova Persei, a discovery that led to the recognition that novas were exploding stars. Earlier, he had won considerable notoriety by making a series of balloon ascents over Paris to carry out high-altitude meteorological observations, a bold and quite risky exploit at the time.

Yet Flammarion managed to find the time to produce a

lengthy list of books in several fields. His best-known work was *Popular Astronomy* (1880), a widely read account of current scientific knowledge that served as a standard text for several decades. But there was a speculative, even mystic, side to his nature also, one that manifested itself in a series of far-ranging philosophical treatises and works of science fiction and—as his thinking veered deep into spiritualism—eventually caused some undermining of his scientific reputation.

As early as 1858, when he was a sixteen-year-old student at the Paris Observatory, Flammarion wrote a fantastic romance, *Voyage Extatique aux Regions Lunaires.* That adjective "*extatique,*" with its overtones of rapture and trance, gives us some indication of the innate flamboyance of his outlook. A few years later he published two books dealing with the subject of life on other planets. One, *The Plurality of Inhabited Worlds,* was scientific in tone, but its companion volume, *The Inhabitants of the Other World,* was a flight of fantasy, purporting to be revelations communicated through a medium, Mlle. Huet.

These two were followed in 1864 by yet another speculative work, *Real and Imaginary Worlds,* and then by *Stories of Infinity* (1874), a group of three novellas, the second of which, "Lumen," continued to occupy Flammarion's attention for many years, undergoing several revisions and expansions before appearing in its final book-length form in 1894. *Lumen,* as the novel was also called, consisted of a series of dialogues between Flammarion's protagonist and a disembodied spirit who roved the universe at will. As was true of much of his work, it was a mix of the didactic and the vigorously imaginative, offering an accurate and reliable account of contemporary astronomical knowledge intermingled with fervent and uninhibited occultist rumination.

We find this mix in his novel *Omega* as well. What begins as a professional astronomer's sober and barely fictionalized examination of one plausible way in which the world might be destroyed, with an excursion into discussions of various other modes of planetary catastrophe, is transformed most unexpectedly, midway through, into a startling journey toward the end of time, carried off with the sort of visionary gusto that would not be managed again until the advent of Olaf Stapledon's *Last and First Men* nearly forty years later.

Beyond much doubt it was his work as an astronomer, in particular his research on novas and supernovas, that drew Flammarion's mind into these apocalyptic realms of eschatological thought. Long before his own studies of Nova Persei, he had made himself familiar with Tycho Brahe's work on the supernova event of 1572 and that of Brahe's successor Kepler on the one of 1604. It was Brahe who had predicted that the new star that we identify with his name would bring "a period of wars, seditions, captivity, death of princes, and destruction of cities, together with dryness and fiery meteors in the air, pestilence, and venomous snakes." Kepler too, noting that *his* supernova could be seen ominously blazing overhead in vivid colors alongside Jupiter, Saturn, and Mars—at that time clustered ominously close together in the sky—saw its advent as a sinister astrological portent.

Flammarion, of course, understood that the explosion of distant stars could have no impact on contemporary terrestrial events, but his mind was well attuned to the possibility of cosmic catastrophes of all sorts. In the opening chapters of *Omega* he provides a calm, rational, almost dispassionate account of the sudden appearance in the night sky of a mysterious and terrifying celestial intruder: a great green comet, which is gradually discovered to be heading straight toward our world.

The scenes leading toward the arrival of the comet are handled with the kind of scientific accuracy one would expect from the author of the era's most highly regarded popular text on astronomy. Now and again Flammarion deviates into scientific fantasy. The establishment of an observatory near the summit of Mount Everest, protected from the fierce weather "by newly discovered processes of electro-chemistry," seems quaintly optimistic today, as does the notion that over the course of nine or ten generations astronomers would become acclimated to the rarefied atmosphere they would encounter up there. And his casual assertion of the existence of intelligent beings on Mars would not be shared by any of his professional colleagues today.

But, by and large, Flammarion's closely detailed account of the discovery of the comet and its dire trajectory maintains sober contact with the scientific knowledge of his day, and the little science-fictional touches with which he embellishes his picture of the world of the twenty-fifth century (his references to "electric air-ships," for example, and to the "telephonoscopes" with which messages from the Martians are received) are handled in a charmingly musty way. Flammarion sees the telephone as a truly wondrous device and makes his twenty-fifth-century people dependent on it for all kinds of long-distance communication. (He does not seem to have envisioned the coming of wireless transmission, although he would no doubt feel a certain vindication upon learning of the way the Internet has reestablished the telephone's central place in our communications net after decades of dominance by radio and television.)

His narrative mode in these chapters is wholly expository—dry, even. He eschews the fictional techniques of such storytellers as Verne and Wells, makes only the most minimal gestures toward creating realistic characters and providing naturalistic dialog, and devotes himself almost exclusively to a straightforward technical account of the oncoming disaster. Our first indication that he has something more unusual in mind than an arid pseudo-scientific narrative turns up in the fifth chapter. The debate of the scientists over the perils posed by the approaching comet suddenly gives way to a discussion among theologians of the resurrection of the dead, and the archbishop of Paris rises to offer an astonishing biochemical rationale for the validity of a belief that, in the last days of Earth, all who have ever existed will return to physical life. Here we meet Flammarion the scientific mystic for the first time in the story, but not the last. It is his obsession with the immortality of the spirit that will carry us the rest of the distance in what had previously appeared to be nothing more than an elaborately conceived catastrophe novel deeply rooted in scientific reality.

For the comet comes, it does its work, and though the French title of the novel, *La Fin du Monde*, has led us to think that the author's intent is to provide a portrayal of the destruction of civilization at the hands of an errant celestial body, that is not what happens. But Flammarion does abandon his dispassionate scientific tone to give us some exceedingly splendid descriptive passages full of science-fictional passion and fervor.

> During the night of July 13–14, the comet spread over nearly the entire sky, and whirlwinds of fire could be seen by the naked eye. . . . The appearance was that of an army of flaming meteors, in whose midst the flashing lightning produced the effect of a furious combat. The burning star had a revolution of its own, and seemed to be convulsed with pain, like a living thing. Immense jets of flame issued from various centers, some of a greenish hue, others red as blood, while the most brilliant were of a dazzling whiteness. . . . The comet itself emitted a light far different from the sunlight reflected by the enveloping vapors; and its flames, shooting forth in ever-increasing volume, gave it the appearance of a monster, precipitating itself upon the earth to devour it.

Flammarion's special effects are not merely horrific but often masterly in the surprise they engender. "Perhaps the most striking feature of this spectacle was the absence of all sound. At Paris, as elsewhere, during that eventful night, the crowd instinctively maintained silence, spellbound by an indescribable fascination, endeavoring to catch some echo of the celestial thunder—but not a sound was heard."

The hour of collision approaches. A green moon rises. The atmosphere of Earth grows drier and warmer. Breathing becomes almost impossible. The eerie silence deepens. Then the comet becomes visible in the west, "a vaporous, scarlet sun, with flames of yellow and green, like immense extended wings." The horizon is illuminated by a ring of bluish flame. The vault of heaven is rent asunder; greenish fire belches forth; a rain of shooting stars begins. And then—then—

Then Flammarion's real story begins. For the book is scarcely past its halfway point when the comet comes, frightens everyone half to death, and passes on into space, leaving the people of Earth startled but largely unharmed. Now, most unexpectedly, he launches into a far-reaching tale spanning millions of years and carrying the tale toward his real purpose, which is not to tell a simple tale of a violent random event that destroys the Earth, but rather to explore ultimate eschatological concepts, the persistence of life, even its meaning, and the destiny that awaits all living things at the end of time.

It becomes clear, as these later chapters unfold, that the thirty-page essayistic digression on millenarian fantasy, resurrectionist theology, and the inevitability of the world's end with which Flammarion interrupts his story just prior to the comet's arrival is no mere padding, but is in fact the heart of Flammarion's book. The comet is, in fact, incidental. He has cast his mind forward across all the remaining span of time, and wants to tell us about it. And tell us he does, in a way that no writer had done before, and few other than Olaf Stapledon have done since. "All is eternal, and merges into the divine," Flammarion declares, and as he does, he carries us very far from the simple-minded world of Hollywood catastrophe movies.

The influence of Flammarion's astonishing novel on later writers is not difficult to trace. Certainly we see it in Stapledon, whose great epic *Last and First Men* (1930) traverses much of Flammarion's domain and then goes far beyond it in the course of providing a history of the next two billion years. In H.G. Wells' *The Time Machine* (1895), Flammarion's touch can plainly be seen in the melancholy view of Earth's last inhabitant, thirty million years hence, a monstrous crab moving slowly along a barren beach under a reddened sun and a lurid sky, as the universe freezes toward its final moment. And Wells' "The Star" (1897) must surely have been written not long after a reading of *Omega*, for it is little more than a retelling of the first section of Flammarion's tale in a few thousand words, complete to the dispassionate journalistic tone and the observations of the Martian astronomers. In 1906 Wells returned to the theme yet again in his novel *In the Days of the Comet*, handling it more originally this time, but showing a clear debt to Flammarion in its view of the coming of the comet as a fundamentally benign event.

Another who must certainly have read Flammarion is his compatriot Jules Verne, who very likely drew on the latter sections of *Omega* for his novella, "The Eternal Adam" (1905). In this story, written late in Verne's career, Verne espouses a cyclical view of the world. Earth is destroyed by a calamitous earthquake and flood, but the continent of Atlantis wondrously emerges from the depths to provide a new home for the human race, which after thousands of years of toil rebuilds civilization. We are given a glimpse, finally, of a venerable scholar of the far future looking back through the archives of humanity, "bloodied by the innumerable hardships suffered by those who had gone before him," and coming, "slowly, reluctantly, to an intimate conviction of the eternal return of all things."

The eternal return! That phrase of Verne's links his story to the core of Flammarion's own belief that our own little epoch is "an imperceptible wave on the immense ocean of the ages" and that mankind's destiny is, as we see in his closing pages, to be born again and again into universe after universe, each to pass on in its turn and be replaced, for time goes on forever and there can be neither end nor beginning. Flammarion has swept his readers far beyond the simple and sensationalistic oh-my-God-everything-is-going-to-get-smashed story that he seems originally to be offering, into realms of wondrous speculation. It is a remarkable conclusion to a remarkable book.

By Jean Paul Laurens.

OMEGA:

THE LAST DAYS OF THE WORLD.

CHAPTER I.

THE magnificent marble bridge which unites the Rue
de Rennes with the Rue de Louvre, and which, lined
with the statues of celebrated scientists and philosophers,
emphasizes the monumental avenue leading to the new
portico of the Institute, was absolutely black with people.
A heaving crowd surged, rather than walked, along the

quays, flowing out from every street and pressing forward
toward the portico, long before invaded by a tumultuous
throng. Never, in that barbarous age preceding the constitution of the United States of Europe, when might was
greater than right, when military despotism ruled the
world and foolish humanity quivered in the relentless
grasp of war—never before in the stormy period of a
great revolution, or in those feverish days which accompanied a declaration of war, had the approaches of the
house of the people's representatives, or the Place de la
Concorde presented such a spectacle. It was no longer
the case of a band of fanatics rallied about a flag, marching
to some conquest of the sword, and followed by a throng
of the curious and the idle, eager to see what would happen; but of the entire population, anxious, agitated, terrified, composed of every class of society without distinction,
hanging upon the decision of an oracle, waiting feverishly
the result of the calculations which a celebrated astronomer was to announce that very Monday, at three o'clock,
in the session of the Academy of Sciences. Amid the flux
of politics and society the Institute survived, maintaining
still in Europe its supremacy in science, literature and art.
The center of civilization, however, had moved westward,
and the focus of progress shone on the shores of Lake
Michigan, in North America.

This new palace of the Institute, with its lofty domes
and terraces, had been erected upon the ruins remaining

after the great social revolution of the international an-archists who, in 1950, had blown up the greater portion of the metropolis as from the vent of a crater.

THE STREETS OF PARIS BY NIGHT.

On the Sunday even-ing before, one might have seen from the car of a balloon all Paris abroad upon the boule-vards and public squares, circulating slowly and as if in despair, without interest in anything. The gay aerial ships no longer cleaved the air; aeroplanes and aviators had all ceased to circu-late. The aerial stations upon the summits of the towers and build-ings were empty and de-serted. The course of human life seemed ar-rested, and anxiety was depicted upon every face. Strangers addressed each other without hesitation; and but one question fell from pale and trembling lips: "Is it then true?" The most deadly pestilence would have carried far less terror to the heart than the astronomical prediction on every tongue ; it would have made fewer victims, for already, from some unknown cause, the death-rate was increasing. At every instant one felt the electric shock of a terrible fear.

A few, less dismayed, wished to appear more confident, and sounded now and then a note of doubt, even of hope, as : "It may prove a mistake ;" or, "It will pass on one side ;" or, again : "It will amount to nothing ; we shall get off with a fright," and other like assurances.

But expectation and uncertainty are often more terrible than the catastrophe itself. A brutal blow knocks us down once for all, prostrating us more or less completely. We come to our senses, we make the best of it, we recover, and take up life again. But this was the unknown, the expectation of something inevitable but mysterious, terrible, coming from without the range of experience. One was to die, without doubt, but how ? By the sudden shock of collision, crushed to death ? By fire, the conflagration of a world ? By suffocation, the poisoning of the atmosphere ? What torture awaited humanity ? Apprehension was perhaps more frightful than the reality itself. The mind cannot suffer beyond a certain limit. To suffer by inches, to ask every evening what the morning may bring, is to suffer a thousand deaths. Terror, that terror which congeals the blood in the veins, which annihilates the courage, haunted the shuddering soul like an invisible spectre.

THE OBSERVATORY ON GAURISANKAR.

For more than a month the business of the world had been suspended; a fortnight before the committee of administrators (formerly the chamber and senate) had adjourned, every other question having sunk into insignificance. For a week the exchanges of Paris, London, New York and Pekin, had closed their doors. What was the use of occupying oneself with business affairs, with questions of internal or foreign policy, of revenue or of reform, if the end of the world was at hand? Politics, indeed! Did one even remember to have ever taken any interest in them? The courts themselves had no cases; one does not murder when one expects the end of the world. Humanity no longer attached importance to anything; its heart beat furiously, as if about to stop forever. Every face was emaciated, every countenance discomposed, and haggard with sleeplessness. Feminine coquetry alone held out, but in a superficial, hesitating, furtive manner, without thought of the morrow.

The situation was indeed serious, almost desperate, even in the eyes of the most stoical. Never, in the whole course of history had the race of Adam found itself face to face with such a peril. The portents of the sky confronted it unceasingly with a question of life and death.

But, let us go back to the beginning.

Three months before the day of which we speak, the director of the observatory of Mount Gaurisankar had sent the following telephonic message to the principal observatories of the globe, and especially to that of Paris : *

"A telescopic comet discovered tonight, in 290°, 15′ right ascension, and 21°, 54′ south declination. Slight diurnal motion. Is of greenish hue."

Not a month passed without the discovery of telescopic

---

* For about 300 years the observatory of Paris had ceased to be an observing station, and had been perpetuated only as the central administrative bureau of French astronomy. Astronomical observations were made under far more satisfactory conditions upon mountain summits in a pure atmosphere, free from disturbing influences. Observers were in direct and constant communication by telephone with the central office, whose instruments were used only to verify certain discoveries or to satisfy the curiosity of savants detained in Paris by their sedentary occupation.

comets, and their announcement to the various observatories, especially since the installation of intrepid astronomers in Asia on the lofty peaks of Gaurisankar, Dapsang and Kanchinjinga; in South America, on Aconcagua, Illampon and Chimborazo, as also in Africa on Kilimanjaro, and in Europe on Elburz and Mont Blanc. This announcement, therefore, had not excited more comment among astronomers than any other of a like nature which they were constantly receiving. A large number of observers had sought the comet in the position indicated, and had carefully followed its motion. Their observations had been published in the Neuastronomischenachrichten, and a German mathematician had calculated a provisional orbit and ephemeris.

Scarcely had this orbit and ephemeris been published, when a Japanese scientist made a very remarkable suggestion. According to these calculations, the comet was approaching the sun from infinite space in a plane but slightly inclined to that of the ecliptic, an extremely rare occurrence, and, moreover, would traverse the orbit of Saturn. " It would be exceedingly interesting," he remarked, " to multiply observations and revise the calculation of the orbit, with a view to determining whether the comet will come in collision with the rings of Saturn ; for this planet will be exactly at that point of its path intersected by the orbit of the comet, on the day of the latter's arrival."

A young laureate of the Institute, a candidate for the director- ship for the observatory, acting at once on this sug- gestion, had installed her- self at the tel- ephone office in order to capture on the wing every

THE YOUNG LAUREATE.

message. In less than ten days she had intercepted more than one hundred despatches, and, without losing an instant, had devoted three nights and days to a revision of the orbit as based on this entire series of observations. The result proved that the German com- putor had committed an error in determining the peri- helion distance and that the inference drawn by the Japanese astronomer was inexact in so far as the date of the comet's passage through the plane of the ecliptic was concerned, this date being five or six days earlier than that first announced; but the interest in the problem increased, for the minimum distance of the comet from the earth seemed now less than the Japanese calculator had thought possible. Setting aside for the moment, the question of a collision, it was hoped that the enormous perturbation which would result from the at- traction of the earth and moon would afford a new method of determining with exhaustive precision the mass of both these bodies, and perhaps even throw important light upon the density of the earth's interior. It was, indeed, established that the celestial visitor was moving in a plane nearly coincident with that of the ecliptic, and would pass near the system of Saturn, whose attraction would probably modify to a sensible degree the primitive parabolic orbit, bringing it nearer to the belated planet. But the comet, after traversing the orbits of Jupiter and of Mars, was then to enter exactly that described annually by the earth about the sun. The interest of astronomers was not on this account any the less keen, and the young computor insisted more forcibly than ever upon the importance of numerous and exact observations.

It was at the observatory of Gaurisankar especially that the study of the comet's elements was prosecuted. On this highest elevation of the globe, at an altitude of 8000 meters, among eternal snows which, by newly discovered processes of electro-chemistry, were kept at a distance of several kilometers from the station, towering almost always many hundred meters above the highest clouds, in a pure and rarified atmosphere, the visual power of both the eye and the telescope was increased a hundred fold. The craters of the moon, the satellites of Jupiter, and the phases of Venus could be readily distinguished by the naked eye. For nine or ten generations several families of astronomers had lived upon this Asiatic summit, and had gradually become accustomed to its rare atmosphere. The first comers had succumbed; but science and industry had succeeded in modifying the rigors of the temperature by the storage of solar heat, and acclimatization slowly took place ; as in former times, at Quito and Bogota, where, in the eighteenth and nineteenth centuries, a contented population lived in plenty, and young women might be seen dancing all night long without fatigue ; whereas on Mont Blanc in Europe, at the same elevation, a few steps only were attended with painful respiration. By degrees a small colony was installed upon the slopes of the Himalayas, and, through their researches and discoveries, the observatory had acquired the reputation of being the first in the world. Its principal instrument was the celebrated equatorial of one hundred meters focal length, by whose aid the hieroglyphic signals, addressed in vain for several thousand years by the inhabitants of the planet Mars to the earth, had finally been deciphered.

While the astronomers of Europe were discussing the orbit of the new comet and establishing the precision of the computations which foretold its convergence upon the earth and the collision of the two bodies in space, a new phonographic message was sent out from the Himalayan observatory :

" The comet will soon become visible to the naked eye. Still of greenish hue. Its course is earthward."

The complete agreement between the astronomical data, whether from European, American, or Asiatic sources, could leave no further doubt of their exactness. The daily papers sowed broadcast this alarming news, embellished with sinister comments and numberless interviews in which the most astonishing statements were attributed to scientists. Their only concern was to outdo the ascertained facts, and to exaggerate their bearing by more ·or less fanciful additions. As for that matter, the journals of the world had long since become purely business enterprises. The sole preoccupation of each was to sell every day the greatest possible number of copies. They invented false news, travestied the truth, dishonored men and women, spread scandal, lied without shame, explained the devices of thieves and murderers, published the formulæ of recently invented explosives, imperilled their own readers and betrayed every class of society, for the sole purpose of exciting to the highest pitch the curiosity of the public and of "selling copies."

Everything had become a pure matter of business. For science, art, literature, philosophy, study and research, the press cared nothing. An acrobat, a runner or a jockey, an air-ship or water-velocipede, attained more celebrity in a day than the most eminent scientist, or the most ingenious inventor—for these two classes made no return to the stockholders. Everything was adroitly decked out with the rhetoric of patriotism, a sentiment which still exercised some empire over the minds of men. In short, from every point of view, the pecuniary interests of the publication dominated all considerations of public interest

2

and general progress. Of all this the public had been for
a long time the dupe; but, at the time of which we are
now speaking, it had surrendered to the situation, so that
there was no longer any newspaper, properly speaking,
but only sheets of notices and advertisements of a com-
mercial nature. Neither the first announcement of the
press, that a comet was approaching with a high velocity
and would collide with the earth at a date already determined; nor the second, that the wandering star might
bring about a general catastrophe by rendering the atmosphere irrespirable, had produced the slightest impression;
this two-fold prophecy, if noticed at all by the heedless
reader, had been received with profound incredulity, attracting no more attention than the simultaneous an-

nouncement of the discovery of
the fountain of perpetual youth
in the cellars of the Palais des
Fées on Montmartre (erected on
the ruins of the cathedral of the
Sacré-Cœur).

Moreover, astronomers themselves had not, at first, evinced
any anxiety about the collision,
so far as it affected the fate of
humanity, and the astronomical
journals (which alone retained
any semblance of authority) had

A SHOWER OF STARS.

as yet referred to the subject simply as a computation to be verified. Scientists had treated the problem as one of pure mathematics, regarding it only as an interesting case of celestial mechanics. In the interviews to which they had been subjected they had contented themselves with saying that a collision was possible, even probable, but of no interest to the public.

Meanwhile, a new message was received by telephone, this time from Mount Hamilton in California, which produced a sensation among the chemists and physiologists :

" Spectroscopic observation establishes the fact that the comet is a body of considerable density, composed of several gases the chief of which is carbonic-oxide."

Matters were becoming serious. That a collision with the earth would occur was certain. If astronomers were not especially preoccupied by this fact, accustomed as they were for centuries to consider these celestial conjunctions as harmless : if the most celebrated even of their number had, at last, coldly shown the door to the many beardless reporters constantly importuning them, declaring that this prediction was of no interest to the people at large and was a strictly astronomical question which did not concern them, physicians, on the other hand, had begun to agitate the subject and to discuss gravely, among each other, the possibilities of asphyxia, or poisoning. Less indifferent to public opinion, so far from turning a cold shoulder to the journalists, they had welcomed them, and in a few days the subject suddenly entered upon a new phase. From the domain of astronomy it had passed into that of philosophy, and the name of every well-known or famous physician appeared in large letters on the title-pages of the daily papers; their portraits were reproduced in the illustrated journals, and the formula, "Interviews on the Comet," was to be seen on every hand. Already, even, the variety and diversity of conflicting opinions had created hostile camps, which hurled at each other the most grotesque abuse, and asserted that all physicians were "charlatans eager for notoriety."

In the mean time the director of the Paris observatory having at heart the interests of science, was profoundly disturbed by an uproar which had more than once, on former occasions, singularly misrepresented astronomical facts. He was a venerable old man who had grown gray in the study of the great problems of the constitution of the universe. His utterances were respected by all, and he had decided to make a statement to the press in which he declared that all conjectures, made prior to the technical discussion authorized by the Institute, were premature.

It has been remarked, we believe, that the Paris observatory, always in the van of every scientific movement, by virtue of the labors of its members, and more especially, of improved methods of observation, had become, on the one hand, the sanctuary of theoretical research, and on the

By Jean Paul Laurens.

other the central telephone bureau for stations established at a distance from the great cities on elevations favored by a perfectly transparent atmosphere.

It was an asylum of peace, where perfect concord reigned, where astronomers disinterestedly consecrated their whole lives to the advancement of science, and mutually encouraged each other, without experiencing any of the pangs of envy, each forgetting his own merit to proclaim that of his colleagues. The director set the example, and when he spoke it was in the name of all.

He published a technical discussion, and he was listened to—for a moment. For the question appeared to be no longer one of astronomy. No one denied or disputed the meeting of the comet with the earth. That was a fact which mathematics had rendered certain. The absorbing question now was the chemical constitution of the comet. If the earth, in its passage through it, was to lose the oxygen of its atmosphere, death by asphyxia was inevitable; if, on the other hand, the nitrogen was to combine with the cometary gases, death was still certain; but death preceded by an ungovernable exhilaration, a sort of universal intoxication, a wild delirium of the senses being the necessary result of the extraction of nitrogen from the respirable air and the proportionate increase of oxygen.

The spectroscope indicated especially the presence of carbonic-oxide in the chemical constitution of the comet. The chief point under discussion in the scientific reviews was whether the mixture of this noxious gas with the atmosphere would poison the entire population of the globe, human and animal, as the president of the academy of medicine affirmed would be the case.

Carbonic-oxide! Nothing else was talked of. The spectroscope could not be in error. Its methods were too sure, its processes too precise. Everybody knew that the smallest admixture of this gas with the air we breathe meant a speedy death. Now, a later despatch from the observatory of Gaurisankar had more than confirmed that received from Mount Hamilton. This despatch read:

"The earth will be completely submerged in the nucleus of the comet, whose diameter is already thirty times that of the globe and is daily increasing."

Thirty times the diameter of the earth! Even then, though the comet should pass between the earth and the moon, it would touch them both, since a bridge of thirty earths would span the distance between our world and the moon.

Then, too, during the three months whose history we have recapitulated, the comet had emerged from regions accessible only to the telescope and had become visible to the naked eye. In full view of the earth it hovered now like a threat from heaven among the army of stars. Terror itself, advancing slowly but inexorably, was suspended like a mighty sword above every head. A last effort was made, not indeed to turn the comet from its path—an idea

conceived by that class of visionaries who recoil before
nothing, and who had even imagined that an electric
storm of vast magnitude might be produced by batteries
suitably distributed over that face of the globe which was
to receive the shock—but to examine once more the great
problem under every aspect, and perhaps to reassure the
public mind and rekindle hope by the discovery of some
error in the conclusions which had been drawn, some
forgotten fact in the observations or computations. This
collision might not after all prove so fatal as the pes-
simists had foretold. A general presentation of the
case from every point of view was announced for this
very Monday at the Institute, just four days before the
prophesied moment of collision, which would take place
on Friday, July 13th. The most celebrated astronomer
of France, at that time director of the Paris observatory ;
the president of the academy of medicine, an eminent
physiologist and chemist ; the president of the astronomical society, a skillful mathematician, and other orators
also, among them a woman distinguished for her discoveries in the physical sciences, were among the speakers
announced. The last word had not yet been spoken. Let
us enter the venerable dome and listen to the discussion.

But before doing so, let us ourselves consider this
famous comet which for the time being absorbed every
thought.

THE stranger had emerged slowly from the depths of space. Instead of appearing suddenly, as more than once the great comets have been observed to do,—either because coming into view immediately after their perihelion passage, or after a long series of storms or moonlight nights has prevented the search of the sky by the comet-seekers—this floating star-mist had at first remained in regions visible only to the telescope, and had been watched only by astronomers. For several days after its discovery, none but the most powerful equatorials of the observatories could detect its presence. But the well-informed were not slow to examine it for themselves. Every modern house was crowded with a terrace,

THE STREET TELESCOPES.

partly for the purpose of facilitating aerial embarkations. Many of them were provided with revolving domes. Few well-to-do families were without a telescope, and no home was complete without a library, well furnished with scientific books.

The comet had been observed by everybody, so to speak, from the instant it became visible to instruments of moderate power. As for the laboring classes, whose leisure moments were always provided for, the telescopes set up in the public squares had been surrounded by impatient crowds from the first moment of visibility, and every evening the receipts of these astronomers of the open air had been incredible and without precedent. Many workmen, too, had their own instruments, especially in the provinces, and justice, as well as truth, compels us to acknowledge that the first discoverer of the comet (outside of the professional observers) had not been a man of the world, a person of importance, or an academician, but a plain workman of the town of Soissons, who passed the greater portion of his nights under the stars, and who had succeeded in purchasing out of his laboriously accumulated savings an excellent little telescope with which he was in the habit of studying the wonders of the sky. And it is a notable fact that prior to the twenty-fourth century, nearly all the inhabitants of the earth had lived without knowing where they were, without even feeling the curiosity to ask, like blind men, with no other preoc-

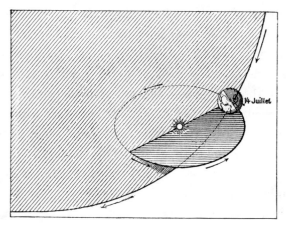

cupation than the satisfaction of their appetites; but within a hundred years the human race had begun to observe and reason upon the universe about them.

To understand the path of the comet through space, it will be sufficient to examine carefully the accompanying chart. It represents the comet coming from infinite space obliquely towards the earth, and afterwards falling into the sun which does not arrest it in its passage toward perihelion. No account has been taken of the perturbation caused by the earth's attraction, whose effect would be to bring the comet nearer to the earth's orbit. All the comets which gravitate about the sun—and they are numerous—describe similar elongated orbits,—ellipses, one of whose foci is occupied by the solar star. The drawing on page 33 gives an idea of the intersections of the cometary and planetary orbits, and the orbit of the earth about the sun. On studying these intersections, we perceive that a collision is neither an impossible nor an abnormal event.

The comet was now visible to the naked eye. On the night of the new moon, the atmosphere being perfectly clear, it had been detected by a few keen eyes without the aid of a glass, not far from the zenith near the edge of the milky way to the south of the star Omicron in the con stellation of Andromeda, as a pale nebula, like a puff of very light smoke, quite small, almost round, slightly elongated in a direction opposed to that of the sun—a gaseous elongation, outlining a rudimentary tail. This, indeed, had been its appearance since its first discovery by the telescope. From its inoffensive aspect no one could have suspected the tragic role which this new star was to play in the history of humanity. Analysis alone indicated its march toward the earth.

But the mysterious star approached rapidly. The very next day the half of those who searched for it had detected it, and the following day only the near-sighted, with eye-glasses of insufficient power, had failed to make it out. In less than a week every one had seen it. In all the public squares, in every city, in every village, groups were to be seen watching it, or showing it to others.

Day by day it increased in size. The telescope began to distinguish distinctly a luminous nucleus. The excitement increased at the same time, invading every mind.

THE COMET AS SEEN AT PARIS.

When, after the first quarter and during the full moon, it appeared to remain stationary and even to lose something of its brilliancy, as it had been expected to grow rapidly larger, it was hoped that some error had crept into the computations, and a period of tranquillity and relief followed. After the full moon the barometer fell rapidly. A violent storm-center, coming from the Atlantic, passed north of the British Isles. For twelve days the sky was entirely obscured over nearly the whole of Europe.

Once more the sun shone in purified atmosphere, the clouds dissolved and the blue sky reappeared pure and unobscured; it was not without emotion that men waited for the setting of the sun—especially as several aerial expeditions had succeeded in rising above the cloud-belts, and aeronauts had asserted that the comet was visibly larger. Telephone messages sent out from the mountains of Asia and America announced also its rapid approach. But great was the surprise when at nightfall every eye was turned heavenward to seek the flaming star. It was no longer a comet, a classic comet such as one had seen before, but an aurora borealis of a new kind, a gigantic celestial fan, with seven branches, shooting into space seven greenish streamers, which appeared to issue from a point hidden below the horizon.

No one had the slightest doubt but that this fantastical aurora borealis was the comet itself, a view confirmed by the fact that the former comet could not be found any-where among the starry host. The apparition differed, it is true, from all popularly known cometary forms, and the radiating beams of the mysterious visitor were, of all forms, the least expected. But these gaseous bodies are so remarkable, so capricious, so various, that everything is possible. Moreover, it was not the first time that a comet had presented such an aspect. Astronomy contained among its records that of an immense comet observed in 1744, which at that time had been the subject of much discussion, and whose picturesque delineation, made de visu by the astronomer Chèzeaux, at Lausanne, had given it a wide celebrity. But even if nothing of this nature had been seen before, the evidence of one's eyes was indubitable.

Meanwhile, discussions multiplied, and a veritable astronomical tournament was commenced in the scientific reviews of the entire world—the only journals which in-

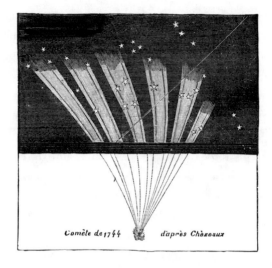

Comète de 1744   *d'après Chèzeaux*

spired any confidence amid the epidemic of buying and selling which had for so long a time possessed humanity. The main question, now that there was no longer any doubt that the star was moving straight toward the earth, was its position from day to day, a question depending upon its velocity. The young computor of the Paris observatory, chief of the section of comets, sent every day a note to the official journal of the United States of Europe.

A very simple mathematical relation exists between the velocity of every comet and its distance from the sun. Knowing the former one can at once find the latter. In fact the velocity of the comet is simply the velocity of a planet multiplied by the square root of two. Now the velocity of a planet, whatever its distance, is determined by Kepler's third law, according to which the squares of the times of revolution are to each other as the cubes of the distances. Nothing evidently, can be more simple. Thus, for example, the magnificent planet, Jupiter, moves about the sun with a velocity of 13,000 meters per second. A comet at this distance moves, therefore, with the above-mentioned velocity, multiplied by the square root of two, that is to say by the number 1.4142. This velocity is consequently 18,380 meters per second.

The planet Mars revolves about the sun at the rate of 24,000 meters per second. At this distance the comet's velocity is 34,000 meters per second.

The mean velocity of the earth in its orbit is 29,-460 meters per second, a little less in June, a little more in December. In the neighborhood of the earth, therefore, the velocity of the comet is 41,660 meters, independently of the acceleration which the earth might occasion.

These facts the laureate of the Institute called to the attention of the public which, moreover, already possessed some general notions upon the theory of celestial mechanics.

When the threatening star arrived at a distance from the sun equal to that of Mars, the popular fear was no longer a vague apprehension; it took definite form, based, as it was, upon the exact knowledge of the

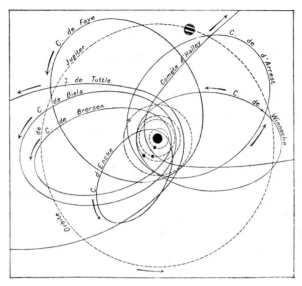

comet's rate of approach. Thirty-four thousand meters per second meant 2040 kilometers per minute, or 122,-400 kilometers per hour!

As the distance of the orbit of Mars from that of the earth is only 76,000,000 of kilometers, at the rate of 122,400 kilometers an hour, this distance would be covered in 621 hours, or about twenty-six days. But, as the comet approached the sun, its velocity would increase, since at the distance of the earth its velocity would be 41,660 meters per second. In virtue of this increase of speed, the distance between the two orbits would be traversed by a comet in 558 hours, or in twenty-three days, six hours.

3

But the earth at the moment of meeting with the comet, would not be exactly at that point of its orbit intersected by a line from the comet to the sun, because the former was not advancing directly toward the latter; the collision, therefore, would not take place for nearly a week later, namely: at about midnight on Friday, the 13th of July. It is unnecessary to add that under such circumstances the usual arrangements for the celebration of the national fête of July 14th had been forgotten. National fête! No one thought of it. Was not that date far more likely to mark the universal doom of men and things? As to that, the celebration by the French of the anniversary of that famous day had lasted—with some exceptions, it is true—for more than five centuries: even among the Romans anniversaries had never been observed for so long a period, and it was generally agreed that the 14th of July had outlived its usefulness.

It was now Monday, the 8th of July. For five days the sky had been perfectly clear, and every night the fan-like comet hovered in the sky depths, its head, or nucleus, distinctly visible and dotted with luminous points which might well be solid bodies several kilometers in diameter, and which, according to the calculations, would be the first to strike the earth, the tail being in a direction away from the sun and in the present instance behind and obliquely situated with refer-

ence to the direction of motion. The new star blazed
in the constellation of Pisces. According to observations taken on the preceding evening, July 8th, its exact position was: right ascension, 23h., 10m., 32s.; declination north, 7°, 36′, 4″. The tail lay entirely across
the constellation of Pegasus. The comet rose at 9h.,
49m. and was visible all night long.

During the lull of which we have spoken, a change
in public opinion had occurred. From a series of retro-
spective calculations an astronomer had proved that the
earth had already on several occasions encountered comets, and that each time the only result had been a
harmless shower of shooting stars. But one of his colleagues had replied that the present comet could not
in any sense be compared to a swarm of meteors, that
it was gaseous, with a nucleus composed of solid bodies
and he had in this connection recalled the observations
made upon a comet famous in history, that of 1811.

This comet of 1811 justified, in a certain respect, a
real apprehension. Its dimensions were recalled to
mind: its length of 180,000,000 kilometers, that is to
say, a distance greater than that of the earth from the
sun; and the width of its tail at its extreme point,
24,000,000 kilometers. The diameter of its nucleus
measured 1,800,000 kilometers, forty thousand times that
of the earth, and its nebulous and remarkably regular
elliptical head was a spot brilliant as a star, having

itself a diameter of no less than 200,000 kilometers. The spot appeared to be of great density. It was observed for sixteen months and twenty-two days. But the most remarkable feature of this comet was the immense development to which it attained without approaching very close to the sun ; for it did not reach a point nearer than 150,000,000 kilometers, and thus remained more than 170,000,000 kilometers from the earth. As the size of comets increases as they near the sun, if this one had experienced to a greater degree the solar action, its appearance would certainly have been still more wonderful, and, doubtless, terrifying to the observer. And as its mass was far from insignificant, if it had fallen directly into the sun, its velocity, accelerated to the rate of five or six hundred thousand meters per second at the moment of collision, might, by the transformation of mechanical energy into thermal energy, have suddenly increased the solar radiations to such a degree as to have utterly destroyed in a few days every trace of vegetable and animal life upon the earth.

A physicist, indeed, had made this curious remark, that a comet of the same size as that of 1811, or greater, might thus bring about the end of the world without actual contact, by a sort of expulsion of solar light and heat, analogous to that observed in the case of temporary stars. The impact would, indeed, give rise to a quantity of heat six times as great as that which would be produced by the combustion of a mass of coal equal to the mass of the comet.

It had been shown that if such a comet in its flight, instead of falling into the sun, should collide with our planet, the end of the world would be by fire. If it collided with Jupiter it would raise the temperature of that globe to such a point as to restore to it its lost light, and to make it for a time a sun again, so that the earth would be lighted by two suns, Jupiter becoming a sort of minor night-sun, far brighter than the moon, and shining by its own light—of a ruby-red or garnet color, revolving about the earth in twelve years. A nocturnal sun! That is to say, no more real night for the earth.

The most classical astronomical treatises had been consulted; chapters on comets written by Newton, Halley, Maupertuis, Lalande, Laplace, Arago, Faye, Newcomb, Holden, Denning, Robert Ball, and their successors, had been re-read. The opinion of Laplace had made the deepest impression and his language had been textually cited: " The earth's axis and rotary motion changed; the oceans abandoning their old-time beds, to rush toward the new equator; the majority of men and animals overwhelmed by this universal deluge, or destroyed by the violent shock; entire species an-nihilated; every monument of human industry overthrown; such are the disasters which might result from collision with a comet."

Thus discussion, researches into the past, calculations, conjectures succeeded each other. But that which made the deepest impression on every mind was first that, as proved by observation, the present comet had a nucleus of considerable density, and second, that carbonic-oxide gas was unquestionably the chief chemical constituent. Fear and terror resumed their sway. Nothing else was thought of, or talked about, but the comet. Already inventive minds sought some way, more or less practicable, of evading the danger. Chemists pretended to be able to preserve a part of the oxygen of the atmosphere. Methods were devised for the isolation of this gas from the nitrogen and its storage in immense vessels of glass hermetically sealed. A clever pharmacist asserted that he had condensed it in pastiles, and in a fortnight expended eight millions in advertising. Thus commerce made capital out of everything, even universal death. All hope was not, however, abandoned. People disputed, trembled, grew anxious, shuddered, died even—but hoped on.

The latest news was to the effect that the comet, developing, as it approached the thermal and electric influences of the sun, would have at the moment of impact a diameter sixty-five times that of the earth, or 828,000 kilometers.

It was in the midst of this state of general anxiety
that the session of the Institute, whose utterance was
awaited as the last word of an oracle, was opened.

The director of the observatory of Paris was naturally to be the first speaker; but what seemed to excite the greatest interest in the public was the opinion
of the president of the academy of medicine on the
probable effects of carbonic-oxide. The president of
the geological society of France was also to make an
address, and the general object of the session was to
pass in review all the possible ways in which our
earth might come to an end. Evidently, however, the
discussion of its collision with the comet would hold
the first place.

As we have just seen, the threatening star hung
above every head; everybody could see it; it was
growing larger day by day; it was approaching with
an increasing velocity; it was known to be at a distance of only 17,992,000 kilometers, and that this distance would be passed
over in five days. Every
hour brought this menac-
ing hand, ready to strike,
149,000 kilometers near-
er. In six days anxious
humanity would breathe
freely—or not at all.

FRIGHTENED WATCHERS.

A GROUP OF LISTENERS.

CHAPTER III.

NEVER, within the history of man, had the immense hemicycle, constructed at the end of the twentieth century, been invaded by so compact a crowd. It would have been mechanically impossible for another person to force an entrance. The amphitheater, the boxes, the tribunes, the galleries, the aisles, the stairs, the corridors, the doorways, all, to the very steps of the platform, were filled with people, sitting or standing. Among the audience were the president of the United States of Europe, the director of the French republic, the directors of the Italian and Iberian republics, the chief ambassador of India, the ambassadors of the British, German, Hungarian and Muscovite republics, the king of the Congo, the president of the committee of administrators, all the ministers, the prefect of the international exchange, the cardinal-archbishop of Paris, the director-general of telephones, the president of the council of aerial navigation and electric roads, the director of the international bureau of time, the principal astronomers, chemists, physiologists and physicians of France, a large number of state officials (formerly called deputies or senators), many celebrated writers and artists, in a word, a rarely assembled galaxy of the representatives of science, politics, commerce, industry, literature and every sphere of human activity. The platform was occupied by the president, vice-presidents, permanent secretaries and orators of the day, but they did not wear, as formerly, the green coat and chapeau or the old-fashioned sword, they were dressed simply in civil costume, and for two centuries and a half every European decoration had been suppressed ; those of central Africa, on the contrary, were of the most brilliant description.

Domesticated monkeys, which for more than half a century had filled every place of service—impossible otherwise to provide for—

A DOMESTICATED MONKEY.

stood at the doors, in conformity to the regulations, rather than to verify the cards of admission; for long before the hour fixed upon every place had been occupied.

The president opened the session as follows (it is needless to remind the reader that the language of the xxxvth century is here translated into that of the xıxth):

"Ladies and gentlemen: You all know the object for which we are assembled. Never, certainly, has humanity passed through such a crisis as this. Never, indeed, has this historic room of the twentieth century contained such an audience. The great problem of the end of the world has been for a fortnight the single object of discussion and study among savants. The results of their discussions and researches are now to be announced. Without further preamble I give place to the director of the observatory."

The astronomer immediately arose, holding a few notes in his hand. He had an easy address, an agreeable voice, and a pleasant countenance. His gestures were few and his expression pleasing. He had a broad forehead and a magnificent head of curling, white hair framed his face. He was a man of learning and of culture, as well as of science, and his whole personality inspired both sympathy and respect. His temperament was evidently optimistic, even under circumstances of great peril. Scarcely had he begun to speak when the mournful and anxious faces before him became suddenly calm and reassured.

"Ladies," he began, "I address myself first to you, begging you not to tremble in this way before a danger which may well be less terrible than it seems. I hope presently to convince you, by the arguments which I shall have the honor to lay before you, that the comet, whose approach is expected by the entire race, will not involve the total ruin of the earth. Doubtless, we may, and should, expect some catastrophe, but as for the end of the world, really, everything would lead us to believe that it will not take place in this manner. Worlds die of old age, not by accident, and, ladies, you know better than I that the world is far from being old.

"Gentlemen, I see before me representatives of every social sphere, from the highest to the most humble. Before a danger so apparent, threatening the destruction of all life, it is not surprising that every business operation should be absolutely suspended. Nevertheless, as for myself, I confess that if the bourse was not closed, and if I had never had the misfortune to be interested in speculation, I should not hesitate to-day to purchase securities which have fallen so low."

This sentence was finished before a noted American Israelite — a prince of finance—director of the journal The Twenty-fifth Century, occupying a seat on one of the upper steps of the amphitheater, forced his way, one hardly knows how, through the rows of benches, and rolled like a ball to the corridor leading to an exit, through which he disappeared.

After the momentary interruption caused by this unexpected sequel to a purely scientific remark, the orator resumed:

"Our subject," he said, "may be considered under three heads: 1. Is the collision of the comet with the earth certain? If this question is answered in the affirmative, we shall

THE PRINCE OF FINANCE LEAVING THE INSTITUTE.

have to examine: 2. The nature of the comet, and, 3, the possible effects of a collision. I have no need to remind so intelligent an audience as this that the prophetic words 'End of the world,' so often heard today, signify solely 'End of the earth,' which moment indeed, of all others, has the most interest for us.

"If we are able to answer the first question in the

negative, it will be quite superfluous to consider the other two, which would become of secondary interest.

" Unfortunately, I must admit that the calculations of the astronomers are in this case, as usual, entirely correct. Yes, the comet will strike the earth, and, doubtless, with maximum force, since the impact will be direct. The velocity of the earth is 29,400 meters per second; that of the comet is 41,660 meters, plus the acceleration due to the attraction of our planet. The initial velocity of contact, therefore, will be 72,000 meters per second. The collision, is inevitable, with all its consequences, if the impact of the comet is direct; but it will be slightly oblique. But do not for this reason, take matters so to heart. In itself the collision proves nothing. If it were announced, for example, that a railway train was to encounter a swarm of flies, this prediction would not greatly trouble the traveller. It may well be that the collision of our earth with this nebulous star will be of the same nature.

" Permit me now to examine, calmly, the two remaining questions.

" First, what is the nature of the comet? That everyone knows already ; it is a gas whose principal constituent is carbonic-oxide. Invisible under ordinary conditions, at the temperature of stellar space (273 degrees below zero), this gas is in a state of vapor,

even of solid particles. The comet is saturated with
them. I shall not in this matter dispute in the least
the discoveries of science."

This confession deepened anew the painful expression on the faces of most of the audience, and here a
long sigh was drawn.

" But, gentlemen," resumed the astronomer, "until
one of our eminent colleagues of the section of physiology, or of the academy of medicine, deigns to prove
for us that the density of the comet is sufficient to
admit of its penetration into our atmosphere, I do not
believe that its presence is likely to exert a fatal influence upon human life. I say is likely, for it is
not possible to affirm this with certainty, although the
probability is very great. One might perhaps wager a
million to one. In any case, only those affected with
weak lungs will be victims. It will be a simple influenza, which may increase three or five-fold the daily
death rate.

" If, however, as the telescope and camera agree in
indicating, the nucleus contains large mineral masses,
probably of a metallic nature, uranolites, measuring
several kilometers in diameter, and weighing some millions of tons, one cannot but admit that the localities
where these masses will fall, with the velocity referred
to a moment ago, would be utterly destroyed. Let us
observe, however, that three-fourths of the globe is

" A FEW CITIES IN ASHES CANNOT ARREST THE HISTORY OF HUMANITY."

covered with water. Here again is a contingency, not so important doubtless as the first, but, nevertheless, in our favor; these masses may perhaps fall into the sea, forming possibly new islands of foreign origin, bringing in any case elements new to science, and, it may be, germs of unknown life; Geodesy would in this case be interested, and the form and rotary movement of the earth might be modified. Let us note also that not a few deserts mark the earth's surface. Danger exists, assuredly, but it is not overwhelming.

"Besides these masses and these gases, perhaps also the bolides of which we were speaking, coming in clouds, will kindle conflagrations at various places on the continents; dynamite, nitroglycerine, panclastite and royalite would be playthings in comparison with what may overtake us, but this does not imply a universal cataclysm ; a few cities in ashes cannot arrest the history of humanity.

" You see, gentlemen, from this methodical examination of the three points before us, it follows that the danger, while it exists, and is even imminent, is not so great, so overwhelming, so certain, as is asserted. I will even say more : this curious astronomical event, which sets so many hearts beating and fills with anxiety so many minds, in the eyes of the philosopher scarcely changes the usual aspect of things. Each one of us must some day die, and this certainty does not prevent us from living tranquilly. Why should the apprehension of a somewhat more speedy death disturb the serenity of so many of us? Is the thought of our dying together so disagreeable? This should prove rather a consolation to our egotism. No, it is the thought that a stupendous catastrophe is to shorten our lives by a few days or years. Life is short, and each clings to the smallest fraction of it ; it would even seem, from what one hears, that each would prefer to see the whole world perish, provided he himself survived, rather than die alone and know the world was saved. This is pure egoism. But, gentlemen, I am firm in the belief that this will be only a partial disaster, of the highest scientific importance, but leaving behind it historians to tell its story. There will be a collision, shock, and local ruin. It will be the history of an earthquake, of a volcanic eruption, of a cyclone."

Thus spoke the illustrious astronomer. The audience appeared satisfied, calmed, tranquillized—in part, at least. It was no longer the question of the absolute end of all things, but of a catastrophe, from which, after all, one would probably escape. Whispered murmurs of conversation were to be heard; people confided to each other their impressions; merchants and politicians even seemed to have perfectly understood the arguments advanced, when, at the invitation of the presiding officer, the president of the academy of medicine was seen advancing slowly toward the tribune.

He was a tall man, spare, slender, erect, with a sallow face and ascetic appearance, and melancholy countenance — bald-headed, and wearing closely-trimmed, gray side-whiskers. His voice had something cadaverous about it, and his whole personality called to mind the undertaker rather than the physician fired with the hope of curing his patients. His estimate of affairs was very different from

" HE WAS A TALL, SPARE MAN."   4

that of the astronomer, as was apparent from the very
first word he uttered.

"Gentlemen," said he, "I shall be as brief as the eminent savant to whom we have just listened, although I
have passed many a night in analyzing, to the minutest
detail, the properties of carbonic-oxide. It is about this
gas that I shall speak to you, since science has demon-
strated that it is the chief constituent of the comet, and
that a collision with the earth is inevitable.

"These properties are terrible ; why not confess it ?
For the most infinitesimal quantity of this gas in the air
we breathe is sufficient to arrest in three minutes the normal action of the lungs and to destroy life.

"Everybody knows that carbonic-oxide (known in
chemistry as CO) is a permanent gas without odor, color
or taste, and nearly insoluble in water. Its density in
comparison with the air is 0.96. It burns in the air with a
blue flame of slight illuminating power, like a funereal fire,
the product of this combustion being carbonic anhydride.

"Its most notable property is its tendency to absorb
oxygen. (The orator dwelt upon these two words with
great emphasis.) In the great iron furnaces, for example,
carbon, in the presence of an insufficient quantity of air,
becomes transformed into carbonic-oxide, and it is subsequently this oxide which reduces the iron to a metallic
state, by depriving it of the oxygen with which it was
combined.

" In the sunlight carbonic-oxide combines with chlorine and gives rise to an oxychlorine ($COCL^2$)—a gas with a disagreeable, suffocating odor.

" The fact which deserves our more serious attention, is that this gas is of the most poisonous character—far more so than carbonic anhydride. Its effect upon the hemoglobin is to diminish the respiratory capacity of the blood, and even in very small doses, by its cumulative effect, hinders, to a degree altogether out of proportion to the apparent cause, the oxygenizing properties of the blood. For example : blood which absorbs from twenty-three to twenty-four cubic centimeters of oxygen per hundred volumes, absorbs only one-half as much in an atmosphere which contains less than one-thousandth part of carbonic-oxide. The one-ten-thousandth part even has a deleterious effect, sensibly diminishing the respiratory action of the blood. The result is not simple asphyxia, but an almost instantaneous blood-poisoning. Carbonic-oxide acts directly upon the blood corpuscles, combining with them and rendering them unfit to sustain life : hematosis, that is, the conversion of venous into arterial blood, is arrested. Three minutes are sufficient to produce death. The circulation of the blood ceases. The black venous blood fills the arteries as well as the veins. The latter, especially those of the brain, become surcharged, the substance of the brain becomes punctured, the base of the tongue, the larynx, the wind-pipe, the bronchial tubes become red with blood, and soon the entire body presents the characteristic purple appearance which results from the suspension of hematosis.

" But, gentlemen, the injurious properties of carbonic-oxide are not the only ones to be feared ; the mere tendency of this gas to absorb oxygen would bring about fatal results. To suppress, nay, even only to diminish oxygen, would suffice for the extinction of the human species. Everyone here present is familiar with that incident which, with so many others, marks the epoch of barbarism, when men assassinated each other legally in the name of glory and of patriotism ; it is a simple episode of one of the English wars in India. Permit me to recall it to your memory :

" One hundred and forty-six prisoners had been confined in a room whose only outlets were two small windows opening upon a corridor ; the first effect experienced by these unfortunate captives was a free and persistent perspiration, followed by insupportable thirst, and soon by great difficulty in breathing. They sought in various ways to get more room and air ; they divested themselves of their clothes ; they beat the air with their hats, and finally resorted to kneeling and rising together at intervals of a few seconds ; but each time some of those whose strength failed them fell and were trampled under the feet of their comrades. Before midnight, that is, during the fourth hour of their confinement, all who were still living,

THE BLACK HOLE OF CALCUTTA.

and who had not succeeded in obtaining purer air at the
windows, had fallen into a lethargic stupor, or a frightful
delirium. When, a few hours later, the prison door was
opened, only twenty-three men came out alive; they were

in the most pitiable state imaginable; every face wearing the impress of the death from which they had barely escaped.

"I might add a thousand other examples, but it would be useless, for doubt upon this point is impossible. I therefore affirm, gentlemen, that, on the one hand, the absorption by the carbonic-oxide of a portion of the atmospheric oxygen, or, on the other, the powerfully toxic properties of this gas upon the vital elements of the blood, alike seem to me to give to the meeting of our globe with the immense mass of the comet—in the heart of which we shall be plunged for several hours—I affirm, I repeat, that this meeting involves consequences absolutely fatal. For my part, I see no chance of escape.

"I have not spoken of the transformation of mechanical motion into heat, or of the mechanical and chemical consequences of the collision. I leave this aspect of the question to the permanent secretary of the academy of sciences and to the learned president of the astronomical society of France, who have made it the subject of important investigations. As for me, I repeat, terrestrial life is in danger, and I see not one only, but two, three and four mortal perils confronting it. Escape will be a miracle, and for centuries no one has believed in miracles."

This speech, uttered with the tone of conviction, in a clear, calm and solemn voice, again plunged the entire audience into a state of mind from which the preceding address had, happily, released them. The certainty of the approaching disaster was painted upon every face ; some had become yellow, almost green ; others suddenly became scarlet and seemed on the verge of apoplexy. Some few among the audience appeared to have retained their self-possession, through scepticism or a philosophic effort to make the best of it. A vast murmur filled the room ; everyone whispered his opinions to his neighbor, opinions generally more optimistic than sincere, for no one likes to appear afraid.

The president of the astronomical society of France rose in his turn and advanced toward the tribune. Instantly every murmur was hushed. Below we give the main points of his speech, including the opening remarks and the peroration :

" Ladies and gentlemen : After the statements which we have just heard, no doubt can remain in any mind as to the certainty of the collision of the comet with the earth, and the dangers attending this event. We must, therefore, expect on Saturday— "

" On Friday," interrupted a voice from the desk of the Institute.

" On Saturday, I repeat," continued the orator, without noticing the interruption, " an extraordinary event, one absolutely unique in the history of the world.

" I say Saturday, although the papers announce that the collision will take place on Friday, because it cannot occur before July 14th. I passed the entire night with my learned colleague in comparing the observations received, and we discovered an error in their transmission."

This statement produced a sensation of relief among the audience; it was like a slender ray of light in the middle of a somber night. A single day of respite is of enormous importance to one condemned to death. Already chimerical projects formed in every mind; the catastrophe was put off; it was a kind of reprieve. It was not remembered that this diversion was of a purely cosmographic nature, relating to the date and not to the fact of the collision. But the least things play an important role in public opinion. So it was not to be on Friday!

"Here," he said, going to the black-board, "are the elements as finally computed from all the observations." The speaker traced upon the black-board the following figures:

Perihelion passage August 11, at 0h., 42m., 44s.

Longitude of perihelion, 52°, 43′, 25″.

Perihelion distance, 0.7607.

Inclination, 103°, 18′, 35″.

Longitude of ascending node, 112°, 54′, 40″.

"The comet," he resumed, "will cross the ecliptic in the direction of the descending node 28 minutes, 23 seconds after midnight of July 14th just as the earth reaches the point of crossing. The attraction of the earth will advance the moment of contact by only thirty seconds.

" The event, doubtless, will be altogether exceptional, but I do not believe either, that it will be of so tragical a nature as has been depicted, or that it can really bring about blood poison or universal asphyxia. It will rather present the appearance of a brilliant display of celestial fire-works, for the arrival in the atmosphere of these solid and gaseous bodies cannot occur without the conversion into heat of the mechanical motion thus destroyed ; a magnificent illumination of the sky will doubtless be the first phenomenon.

" The heat evolved must necessarily be very great. Every shooting star, however small, entering the upper limits of our atmosphere with a cometary velocity, immediately becomes so hot that it takes fire and is consumed. You know, gentlemen, that the earth's atmosphere extends far into space about our planet ; not without limit, as certain hypotheses declare, since the earth turns on its axis and moves about the sun : the mathematical limit is that height at which the centrifugal force engendered by the diurnal rotary motion becomes equal to the weight ; this height is 6.64 times the equatorial radius of the earth, the latter being 6,378,310 meters. The maximum height of the atmosphere, therefore, is 35,973 kilometers.

" I do not here wish to enter into a mathematical discussion. But the audience before me is too well informed not to know the mechanical equivalent of heat. Every body whose motion is arrested produces a quantity of heat expressed in caloric units by mv^2 divided by 8338, in which m is the mass of the body in kilograms and v its velocity in meters per second. For example, a body weighing 8338 kilograms, moving with a velocity of one meter per second, would produce, if suddenly stopped, exactly one heat unit ; that is to say, the quantity of heat necessary to raise one kilogram of water one degree in temperature.

" If the velocity of the body be 500 meters per second, it would produce 250,000 times as much heat, or enough to raise a quantity of water of equal mass from 0° to 30°.

" If the velocity were 5000 meters per second, the heat developed would be 5,000,000 times as great.

" Now, you know, gentlemen, that the velocity with which a comet may reach the earth is 72,000 meters per second. At this figure the temperature becomes five milliards of degrees.

" This, indeed, is the maximum and, I should add, a number altogether inconceivable ; but, gentlemen, let us take the minimum, if it be your pleasure, and let us admit that the impact is not direct, but more or less oblique, and that the mean velocity is not greater than 30,000 meters per second. Every kilogram of a bolide would develop in this case 107,946 heat units before its velocity would be destroyed by the resistance of the air ; in other words, it would generate sufficient heat to raise the temperature of 1079 kilograms of water from 0° to 100°—that is, from the freezing to the boiling point. A uranolite weighing 2000 kilograms would thus, before reaching the earth, develop enough heat to raise the temperature of a column of air, whose cross-section is thirty square meters and whose height is equal to that of our atmosphere, 3000°, or, to raise from 0° to 30° a column whose cross-section is 3000 square meters.

" These calculations, for the introduction of which I crave your pardon, are necessary to show that the immediate consequence of the collision will be the production of an enormous quantity of heat, and, therefore, a considerable rise in the temperature of the air. This is exactly what takes place on a small scale in the case of a single meteorite, which becomes melted and covered superficially by a thin layer of vitrified matter, resembling varnish. But its fall is so rapid that there is not sufficient time for it to become heated to the center ; if broken, its interior is found to be absolutely cold. It is the surrounding air which has been heated.

" One of the most curious results of the analysis which I have just had the honor to lay before you, is that the solid masses which, it is believed, have been seen by the telescope in the nucleus of the comet, will meet with such resistance in traversing our atmosphere that, except in rare instances, they will not reach the earth entire, but in small fragments. There will be a compression of the air in front of the bolide, a vacuum behind it, a superficial heating and incandescence of the moving body, a roar produced by the air rushing into the vacuum, the roll of thunder, explosions, the fall of the denser metallic portions and the evaporation of the remainder. A bolide of sulphur, of phosphorus, of tin or of zinc, would be consumed and dissipated long before reaching the lower strata of our atmosphere. As for the shooting stars, if,

MAKING FOR THE ANTIPODES.

as seems probable, there is a veritable cloud of them, they will only produce the effect of a vast inverted display of fire-works.

" If, therefore, there is any reason for alarm, it is not, in my opinion, because we are to apprehend the penetration of the gaseous mass of carbonic-oxide into our atmosphere, but a rise in temperature, which cannot fail to result from the transformation of mechanical motion into heat. If this be so, safety may be perhaps attained by taking refuge on the side of the globe opposed to that which is to experience the direct shock of the comet, for the air is a very bad conductor of heat."

The permanent secretary of the academy rose in his turn. A worthy successor to the Fontenelles and Aragos of the past, he was not only a man of profound knowledge, but also an elegant writer and a persuasive orator, rising sometimes even to the highest flights of eloquence.

" To the theory which we have just heard," he said, " I have nothing to add ; I can only apply it to the case of some comet already known. Let us suppose, for example, that a comet of the dimensions of that of 1811 should collide squarely with the earth in its path about the sun. The terrestrial ball would penetrate the nebula of the comet without experiencing any very sensible resistance. Admitting that this resistance is very slight, and that the density of the comet's nucleus may be neglected, the passage of the earth through the head of a comet of 1,800,000 kilometers in diameter, would require at least 25,000 seconds—that is, 417 minutes, or six hours, fifty-seven minutes—in round numbers, seven hours—the velocity being 120 times greater than that of a cannon-ball ; and the earth continuing to rotate upon its axis, the collision would commence about six o'clock in the morning.

" Such a plunge into the cometary ocean, however rari-

fied it might be, could not take place without producing
as a first and immediate consequence, by reason of the
thermodynamic principles which have been just called to
your attention, a rise in temperature such that probably
our entire atmosphere would take fire! It seems to me
that in this particular case the danger would be very
serious.

" But it would be a fine spectacle for the inhabitants of
Mars, and a finer one still for those of Venus. Yes, that
would indeed be a magnificent spectacle, analogous to
those we have ourselves seen in the heavens, but far more
splendid to our near neighbors.

" The oxygen of the air would prove insufficient to
maintain the combustion, but there is another gas which
physicists do not often think of, for the simple reason that
they have never found it in their analyses—hydrogen.
What has become of all the hydrogen freed from the soil
these millions of years which have elapsed since prehistoric times? The density of this gas being one-six-
teenth that of the air, it must have ascended, forming a
highly rarified hydrogen envelope above our atmosphere.
In virtue of the law of diffusion of gases, a large part of
this hydrogen would become mixed with the atmosphere,
but the upper air layers must contain a considerable portion
of it. There, doubtless, at an elevation of more than one
hundred kilometers, the shooting stars take fire, and the
aurora borealis is lighted. Notice here that the oxygen

of the air would furnish the carbon of the comet ample
material during collision to feed the celestial fire.

" Thus the destruction of the world will result from the
combustion of the atmosphere. For about seven hours—
probably a little longer, as the resistance to the comet cannot be neglected—there will be a continuous transformation
of motion into a heat. The hydrogen and the oxygen, combining with the carbon of the comet, will take fire. The
temperature of the air will be raised several hundred degrees ; woods, gardens, plants, forests, habitations, edifices,
cities, villages, will all be rapidly consumed ; the sea, the
lakes and the rivers will begin to boil ; men and animals,
enveloped in the hot breath of the comet, will die asphyx-
iated before they are burned, their gasping lungs inhaling
only flame. Every corpse will be almost immediately car-
bonized, reduced to ashes, and in this vast celestial furnace only the heart-rending voice of the trumpet of the
indestructible angel of the Apocalypse will be heard, pro-
claiming from the sky, like a funeral knell, the antique
death-song : ' Solvet sæculum in favilla.' This is what
may happen if a comet like that of 1811 collides with the
earth."

At these words the cardinal-archbishop rose from his
seat and begged to be heard. The astronomer, perceiving
him, bowed with a courtly grace and seemed to await the
reply of his eminence.

" I do not desire," said the latter, " to interrupt the

honorable speaker, but if science announces that the drama of the end of the world is to be ushered in by the destruction of the heavens by fire, I cannot refrain from saying that this has always been the universal belief of the church. 'The heavens,' says St. Peter, 'shall pass away with a great noise, and the elements shall meet with fervent heat, the earth also and the works that are therein shall be burned up.' St. Paul affirms also its renovation by fire, and we repeat daily at mass his words : 'Eum qui venturus est judicare vivos et mortuos et sæculum per ignem.' "

" Science," replied the astronomer, " has more than once been in accord with the prophecies of our ancestors. Fire will first devour that portion of the globe struck by the huge mass of the comet, consuming it before the inhabitants of the other hemisphere realize the extent of the catastrophe ; but the air is a bad conductor of heat, and the latter will not be immediately propagated to the opposite hemisphere.

" If our latitude were to receive the first shock of the comet, reaching us, we will suppose, in summer, the tropic of Cancer, Morocco, Algeria, Tunis, Greece and Egypt would be found in the front of the celestial onset, while Australia, New Caledonia and Oceanica would be the most favored. But the rush of air into this European furnace would be such that a storm more violent than the most frightful hurricane and more formidable even than the air-

5

current which moves continuously on the equator of Jupiter, with a velocity of 400,000 kilometers per hour, would rage from the Antipodes towards Europe, destroying everything in its path. The earth, turning upon its axis, would bring successively into the line of collision, the regions lying to the west of the meridian first blasted. An hour after Austria and Germany it would be the turn of France, then of the Atlantic ocean, then of North America, which would enter somewhat obliquely the dangerous area about five or six hours after France— that is, towards the end of the collision.

" Notwithstanding the unheard-of velocities of the comet and the earth, the pressure cannot be enormous, in view of the extremely rarified state of the matter traversed by the earth ; but this matter, containing so much carbon, is combustible, and at perihelion these bodies are not infrequently seen to shine by their own as well as by reflected light : they become incandescent. What, then, must be the result of a collision with the earth ? The combustion of meteorites and bolides, the superficial fusion of the uranolites which reach the earth's surface on fire, all lead us to believe that the moment of greatest heat will be that of contact, which evidently will not prevent the massive elements forming the nucleus of the comet from crushing the localities where they fall, and perhaps even breaking up an entire continent.

" The terrestrial globe being thus entirely surrounded

DEATH BY SUFFOCATION.

by the cometary mass for nearly seven hours, and revolving in this incandescent gas, the air rushing violently
toward the center of disturbance, the sea boiling and filling the atmosphere with new vapors, hot showers falling
from the sky-cataracts, the storm raging everywhere with
electric deflagrations and lightnings, the rolling of thunder
heard above the scream of the tempest, the blessed light of
former days having been succeeded by the mournful and
sickly gleamings of the glowing atmosphere, the whole
earth will speedily resound with the funeral knell of
universal doom, although the fate of the dwellers in the
Antipodes will probably differ from that of the rest of
mankind.   Instead of being immediately consumed, they
will be stifled by the vapors, by the excess of nitrogen—
the oxygen having been rapidly abstracted—or poisoned
by carbonic-oxide ; the fire will afterwards reduce their
corpses to ashes, while the inhabitants of Europe and
Africa will have been burned alive.

"The well-known tendency of carbonic-oxide to absorb
oxygen will doubtless prove a sentence of instant death
for those farthest from the initial point of the catastrophe.

"I have taken as an example the comet of 1811 ; but I
hasten to add that the present one appears to be far less
dense."

"Is it absolutely sure?" cried a well-known voice (that
of an illustrious member of the chemical society) from one

of the boxes. " Is it absolutely sure the comet is composed chiefly of carbonic-oxide ? Have not the nitrogen lines also been detected in its spectrum ? If it should prove to be protoxide of nitrogen, the consequence of its mixture with our atmosphere might be anæsthesia. Every one would be put to sleep—perhaps forever, if the suspension of the vital functions were to last but a little longer than is the case in our surgical operations. It would be the same if the comet was composed of chloroform or ether. That would be an end calm indeed.

" It would be less so if the comet should absorb the nitrogen instead of the oxygen, for this partial or total absorption of nitrogen would bring about, in a few hours, for all the inhabitants of the earth—for men and women, for the young and the aged—a change of temperament, involving at first nothing disagreeable—a charming sobriety, then gayety, followed by universal joy, a feverish exultation, finally delirium and madness, terminating, in all probability, by the sudden death of every human being in the apotheosis of a wild saturnalia, an unheard-of frenzy of the senses. Would that death be a sad one ? "

" The discussion remains open," replied the secretary. " What I have said of the possible consequences of a collision applies to the direct impact of a comet like that of 1811 ; the one that threatens us is less colossal, and its impact will not be direct, but oblique. In common with the astronomers who have preceded me on this floor, I

am inclined to believe, in this instance, in a mighty display of fire-works."

While the orator was still speaking, a young girl belonging to the central bureau of telephones, entered by a small
door, conducted by a domesticated monkey, and, darting
like a flash to the seat occupied by the president, put into
his hands a large, square, international envelope.   It was
immediately opened, and proved to be a despatch from the
observatory of Gaurisankar.   It contained only the following words :

"The inhabitants of Mars are sending a photophonic
message.   Will be deciphered in a few hours."

"Gentlemen," said the president, " I see several in the
audience consulting their watches, and I agree with them
in thinking that it will be physically impossible for us to
finish in a single session this important discussion, in
which eminent representatives of geology, natural history
and geonomy are yet to take part.   Moreover, the despatch
just read will doubtless introduce new problems.   It is
nearly six o'clock.   I propose that we adjourn to nine
o'clock this evening.   It is probable that we shall have
received, by that time, from Asia the translation of the
message from Mars.   I will also beg the director of the
observatory to maintain constant communication, by telephone, with Gaurisankar.   In case the message is not
deciphered by nine o'clock, the president of the geological
society of France will open the meeting with a statement

of the investigations which he has just finished, on the natural end of the world. Everybody, at this moment, is absorbingly interested in whatever relates to the question of the end of our world, whether this is dependent upon the mysterious portent now suspended above us, or upon other causes, of whatsoever nature, subject to investigation."

CHAPTER IV.

THE multitude stationed without the doors of the Institute had made way for those coming out, every one being eager to learn the particulars of the session. Already the general result had in some way become known, for immediately after the speech of the director of the Paris observatory the rumor got abroad that the collision with the comet would not entail consequences so serious as had been anticipated. Indeed, large posters had just been placarded throughout Paris, announcing the reopening of the Chicago stock exchange. This was an encouraging and unlooked for indication of the resumption of business and the revival of hope.

This is what had taken place. The financial magnate, whose abrupt exit will be remembered by the reader of these pages, after rolling like a ball from the top to the bottom row of the hemicycle, had rushed in an æro-cab to his office on the boulevard St. Cloud, where he had telegraphed to his partner in Chicago that new computations had just been given out by the Institute of France, that the gravity of the situation had been exaggerated, and that the resumption of business was imminent; he urged, therefore, the opening of the central American exchange at any cost, and the purchase of every security offered, whatever its nature. When it is five o'clock at Paris it is eleven in the morning at Chicago. The financier received the despatch from his cousin while at breakfast. He found no difficulty in arranging for the reopening of the exchange and invested several millions in securities. The news of the resumption of business in Chicago had been at once made public, and although it was too late to repeat the same game in Paris, it was possible to prepare new plans for the morrow. The public had innocently believed in a spontaneous and genuine revival of business in America, and this fact, together with the satisfactory impression made by the session of the Institute, was sufficient to rekindle the fires of hope.

No less interest, however, was manifested in the evening session than in that of the afternoon, and but for the exertions of an extra detachment of the French guard it would have been impossible for those enjoying special privileges to gain admission. Night had come, and with it the flaming comet, larger, more brilliant, and more threatening than ever; and if, perhaps, one-half the assembled multitude appeared somewhat tranquillized, the remaining half was still anxious and fearful.

The audience was substantially the same, every one being eager to know at first hand the issue of this general public discussion of the fate of the planet, conducted by accredited and eminent scientists, whether its destruction was to be the result of an extraordinary accident such as now threatened it, or of the natural process of decay. But it was noticed that the cardinal archbishop of Paris was absent, for he had been summoned suddenly to Rome by the Pope to attend an œcumenical council, and had left that very evening by the Paris-Rome-Palermo-Tunis tube.

"Gentlemen," said the president, "the translation of the despatch received at the observatory of Gaurisankar from Mars has not arrived yet, but we shall open the session at once, in order to hear the important communication previously announced, which the president of the geological society, and the permanent secretary of the academy of meteorology, have to make to us."

The former of these gentlemen was already at the desk. His remarks, stenographically reproduced by a young geologist of the new school, were as follows:

"The immense crowd gathered within these walls, the emotion I see depicted upon every face, the impatience with which you await the discussions yet to take place, all, gentlemen, would lead me to refrain from laying before you the opinion which I have formed from my own study of the problem which now excites the interest of the entire world, and to yield the platform to those gifted with an imagination or an audacity greater than mine. For, in my judgment, the end of the world is not at hand, and humanity will have to wait for it several million years — yes, gentlemen, I said *millions*, not thousands.

"You see that I am at this moment perfectly calm, and
that, too, without laying any claim to the sang froid
of Archimedes, who was slain by a Roman soldier at
the siege of Syracuse while calmly tracing geometric figures upon the sand. Archimedes knew the danger and
forgot it; I do not believe in any danger whatever.

"You will not then be surprised if I quietly submit to you the theory of a natural end of the world,
by the gradual levelling of the continents and their slow
submergence beneath the invading waters; but I shall
perhaps do better to postpone for a week this explanation,
as I do not for an instant doubt that we may all, or
nearly all, reassemble here to confer together upon the
great epochs of the natural history of the world."

The orator paused for a moment. The president had risen :
"My dear and honorable colleague," he said, "we are all here
to listen to you. Happily, the pan-
ic of the last few days is partially
allayed, and it is to be hoped that
the night of July 13-14 will pass
like its predecess- ors. Nevertheless,
we are more than ever interested
in all which has any bearing upon
this great problem and we shall listen
to no one with greater pleasure
than to the illus- trious author of
the classic Treat- ise on Geology."

ARCHIMEDES.

"In that case, gentlemen," resumed the president of the geological society of France, "I shall explain to you what, in my judgment, will be the natural end of the world, if, as is probable, nothing disturbs the present course of events; for accidents are rare in the cosmical order.

"Nature does not proceed by sudden leaps, and geologists do not believe in such revolutions or cataclysms; for they have learned that in the natural world everything is subject to a slow process of evolution. The geological agents now at work are permanent ones.

"The destruction of the globe by some great catastrophe is a dramatic conception; far more so, certainly, than that of the action of the forces now in operation, though they threaten our planet with a destruction equally certain. Does not the stability of our continent seem permanent? Except through the intervention of some new agency, how is it possible to doubt the durability of this earth which has supported so many generations before our own, and whose monuments, of the greatest antiquity, prove that if they have come down to us in a state of ruin, it is not because the soil has refused to support them, but because they have suffered from the ravages of time and especially from the hand of man? The oldest historical traditions show us rivers flowing in the same beds as today, mountains rising to the same height; and as for the few river-mouths which have become obstructed, the few land-slides which have occurred here and there, their importance is so slight relatively to the enormous extent of the continents, that it seems gratuitous indeed to seek here the omens of a final catastrophe.

" Such might be the reasoning of one who casts a superficial and indifferent glance upon the external world. But the conclusions of one accustomed to scrutinize closely the apparently insignificant changes taking place about him would be quite different. At every step, however little skilled in observation, he will discover the traces of a perpetual conflict between the external powers of nature and all which rises above the inflexible level of the ocean, in whose depths reign silence and repose. Here, the sea beats furiously against the shore, which recedes slowly from century to century. Elsewhere, mountain masses have fallen, engulfing in a few moments entire villages and desolating smiling valleys. Or, the tropical rains, assailing the volcanic cones, have furrowed them with deep ravines and undermined their walls, so that at last nothing but ruins of these giants remain.

" More silent, but not less efficacious, has been the action of the great rivers, as the Ganges and the Mississippi, whose waters are so heavily laden with solid particles in suspension. Each of these small particles, which trouble the limpidity of their liquid carrier, is a fragment torn from the shores washed by these rivers. Slowly but

THE SEA AT WORK.

STREAM EROSION.

surely their currents bear to the great reservoir of the sea every atom lost to the soil, and the bars which form their deltas are as nothing compared with what the sea receives and hides away in its abysses. How can any reflecting person, observing this action, and knowing that it has been going on for many centuries, escape the conclusion that the rivers, like the ocean, are indeed preparing the final ruin of the habitable world?

"Geology confirms this conclusion in every particular. It shows us that the surface of the soil is being constantly altered over entire continents by variations of temperature, by alterations of drought and humidity, of freezing and thawing, as also by the incessant action of worms and of plants. Hence, a continuous process of dissolution, leading even to the disintegration of the most compact rocks, reducing them to fragments small enough to yield at last to the attraction of gravity, especially when this is aided by running water. Thus they travel, first down the slopes and along the torrent beds, where their angles are worn away and they become little by little transformed into gravel, sand and ooze; then in the rivers which are still able, especially at flood-times, to carry away this broken up material, and to bear it nearer and nearer to their outlets.

"It is easy to predict what must necessarily be the final result of this action. Gravity, always acting, will not be satisfied until every particle subject to its law has attained

6

AT FLOOD-TIME.

the most stable position conceivable. Now, such will be the
case only when matter is in the lowest position possible.
Every surface, must therefore disappear, except the surface
of the ocean, which is the goal of every agency of motion ;
and the material borne away from the crumbling continents must in the end be spread over the bottom of the
sea.   In brief, the final outcome will be the complete levelling of the land, or, more exactly, the disappearance of
every prominence from the surface of the earth.

" In the first place, we readily see that near the river mouths *the final form of the dry land will be that of nearly horizontal plains.* The effect of the erosion produced by running water will be the formation on the water-sheds of a series of sharp ridges, succeeded by almost absolutely horizontal plains, between which no final difference in height greater than fifty meters can exist.

" But in no case can these sharp ridges, which, on this hypothesis, will separate the basins, continue long; for gravity and the action of the wind, filtration and change of temperature, will soon obliterate them. It is thus legitimate to conclude that the end of this erosion of the continents will be *their reduction to an absolute level*, a level differing but little from that at the river outlets."

The coadjutor of the archbishop of Paris, who occupied a seat in the tribune reserved for distinguished functionaries, rose, and, as the orator ceased speaking, added : " Thus will be fulfilled, to the letter, the words of holy writ : ' For the mountains shall depart and the hills be removed.' "

" If, then," resumed the geologist, " nothing occurs to modify the reciprocal action of land and water, we cannot escape the conclusion that every continental elevation is inevitably destined to disappear.

" How much time will this require ?

" The dry land, if spread out in a layer of uniform thickness, would constitute a plateau of about 700 meters

altitude above the sea-level. Admitting that its total area
is 145,000,000 square kilometers, it follows that its volume
is about 101,500,000, or, in round numbers, 100,000,000
cubic kilometers. Such is the large, yet definite mass, with
which the external agencies of destruction must contend.

"Taken together, the rivers of the world may be
considered as emptying, every year, into the sea 23,000
cubic kilometers of water (in other words, 23,000 milliards
of cubic meters). This would give a volume of solid
matter carried yearly to the sea, equal to 10.43 cubic kilometers, if we accept the established ratio of thirty-eight
parts of suspended material in 100,000 parts of water.
The ratio of this amount to the total volume of the dry
land is one to 9,730,000. If the dry land were a level
plateau of 700 meters altitude, it would lose, by fluid

THE RIVERS CEASE TO FLOW.

erosion alone, a slice of about *seven one-hundredths of a millimeter in thickness yearly*, or one millimeter every fourteen years—say *seven millimeters per century*.

"Here we have a definite figure, expressing the actual yearly continental erosion, showing that, if only this erosion were to operate, the entire mass of unsubmerged land would disappear in *less than 10,000,000 years*.

"But rain and rivers are not the only agencies; there are other factors which contribute to the gradual destruction of the dry land:

"First, there is the erosion of the sea. It is impossible to select a better example of this than the Britannic isles; for they are exposed, by their situation, to the onslaught of the Atlantic, whose billows, driven by the prevailing southwest wind, meet with no obstacle to their progress. Now, the average recession of the English coast is certainly less than three meters per century. Let us apply this rate to the sea-coasts of the world, and see what will happen.

"We may proceed in two ways: First, we may estimate the loss in volume for the entire coast-line of the world, on the basis of three centimeters per year. To do this, we should have to know the length of the shore-line and the mean height of the coast. The former is about 200,000 kilometers. As to the present average height of the coasts above the sea, 100 meters would certainly be a liberal estimate. Hence, a recession of three centimeters corresponds to an annual loss of three cubic meters per running meter, or, for the 200,000 kilometers of coast-line, 600,000,000 cubic meters, which is only six-tenths of a cubic kilometer. In other words, the erosion due to the sea would only amount to one-seventeenth that of the rivers.

"It may perhaps be objected, that, as the altitude actually increases from the coast-line toward the interior, the same rate of recession would, in time, involve a greater loss in volume. Is this objection well founded ? No ; for the tendency of the rain and water-courses being, as we have said, to lower the surface-level, this action would keep pace with that of the sea.

"Again, the area of the dry land being 145,000,000 square kilometers, a circle of equal area would have a radius of 6800 kilometers. But the circumference of this circle would be only 40,000 kilometers ; that is to say, the sea could exercise upon the circle but one-fifth the erosive action which it actually does upon the indented outline of our shores. We may, therefore, admit that the erosive action of the sea upon the dry land is *five times greater* than it would be upon an equivalent circular area. Certainly this estimate is a maximum ; for it is logical to suppose that, when the narrow peninsulas have been eaten away by the sea, the ratio of the perimeter to the surface will decrease more and more—that is, the action of the sea will be less effective. In any event, since, at the rate

of three centimeters per year, a radius of 6800 kilometers
would disappear in 226,600,000 years, one-fifth of this
interval, or about 45,000,000 years, would represent the
minimum time necessary for the destruction of the land
by the sea; this would correspond to an intensity of
action scarcely more than *one-fifth* that of the rivers and
rain.

"Taken together, these mechanical causes would, therefore, involve every year a loss in volume of twelve cubic
kilometers, which, for a total of 100,000,000, would bring
about the complete submergence of the dry land in a little
more than *8,000,000 years.*

"But we are far from having exhausted our analysis of the
phenomena in question. Water is not only a mechanical
agent; it is also a powerful dissolvent, far more powerful
than we might suppose, because of the large amount of
carbonic acid which it absorbs either from the atmosphere or from the decomposed organic matter of the soil.
All subterranean waters become charged with substances

THE NILE.

which it has thus chemically abstracted from the minerals
of the rocks through which it percolates.

"River water contains, per cubic kilometer, about 182
tons of matter in solution.   The rivers of the world bring
yearly to the sea, nearly *five cubic kilometers* of such
matter.   The annual loss to the dry land, therefore, from
these various causes, is *seventeen* instead of twelve cubic
kilometers; so that the total of 100,000,000 would disappear, not in eight, but in *a little less than six million
years.*

"This figure must be still further modified.   For we
must not forget that the sediment thus brought to the sea
and displacing a certain amount of water, will cause a rise
of the sea-level, accelerating by just so much the levelling
process due to the wearing away of the continents.

"It is easy to estimate the effect of this new factor.
Indeed, for a given thickness lost by the plateau heretofore
assumed, the sea-level must rise by an amount corresponding to the volume of the submarine deposit, which must
exactly equal that of the sediment brought down.   Calculation shows that, in round numbers, the loss in volume
will be *twenty-four cubic kilometers.*

"Having accounted for an annual loss of twenty-four
cubic kilometers, are we now in a position to conclude
what time will be necessary for the complete disappearance of the dry land, always supposing the indefinite
continuance of present conditions?

" Certainly, gentlemen ; for, after examining the objection which might be made apropos of volcanic eruptions, we find that the latter aid rather than retard the disintegrating process.

" We believe, therefore, that we may fearlessly accept the above estimate of twenty-four cubic kilometers, as a basis of calculation ; and as this figure is contained 4,166,666 times in 100,000,000, which represents the volume of the continents, we are authorized to infer that under the *sole action of forces now in operation*, provided no other movements of the soil occur, *the dry land will totally disappear within a period of about 4,000,000 years.*

" But this disappearance, while interesting to a geologist or a thinker, is not an event which need cause the present generation any anxiety. Neither our children nor our grandchildren will be in a position to detect in any sensible degree its progress.

" If I may be permitted, therefore, to close these remarks with a somewhat fanciful suggestion, I will add that it would be assuredly the acme of foresight to build today a new ark, in which to escape the consequences of this coming universal deluge."

Such was the learnedly developed thesis of the president of the geological society of France. His calm and moderate statement of the secular action of natural forces, opening up a future of 4,000,000 years of life, had allayed the apprehension excited by the comet. The audience

THE WATERS COVERING THE FACE OF THE EARTH.

had become wonderfully tranquillized. No sooner had the orator left the platform and received the congratulations of his colleagues than an animated conversation began on every side. A sort of peace took possession of every mind. People talked of the end of the world as they would of the fall of a ministry, or the coming of the swallows—dispassionately and disinterestedly. A fatality put off 40,000 centuries does not really affect us at all.

But the permanent secretary of the academy of meteorology had just ascended the tribune, and every one gave him at once the strictest attention :

" Ladies and gentlemen : I am about to lay before you a theory diametrically opposed to that of my eminent colleague of the Institute, yet based upon facts no less definite and a process of reasoning no less rigorous.

" Yes, gentlemen, diametrically opposed "—

The orator, gifted with an excellent voice, had perceived the disappointment settling upon every face.

" Oh," he said, " opposed, not as regards the time which nature allots to the existence of humanity, but as to the manner in which the world will come to an end ; for I also believe in a future of several million years.

" Only, instead of seeing the subsidence and complete submergence of the land beneath the invading waters, I foresee, on the contrary, death by drouth, and the gradual diminution of the present water supply of the earth. Some day there will be no more ocean, no more clouds, no

more rain, no more springs, no more moisture, and vegetable as well as animal life will perish, not by drowning, *but
through lack of water.*

"On the earth's surface, indeed, the water of the sea, of
the rivers, of the clouds, and of the springs, is decreasing.
Without going far in search of examples, I would remind
you, gentlemen, that in former times, at the beginning of
the quaternary period, the site now occupied by Paris, with
its 9,000,000 of inhabitants, from Mount Saint-Germain to
Villeneuve-Saint-Georges, was almost entirely occupied by
water; only the hill of Passy at Montmartre and Pere-
Lachaise, and the plateau of Montrouge at the Panthéon
and Villejuif emerged above this immense liquid sheet.
The altitudes of these plateaus have not increased, there
have been no upheavals; it is the water which has
diminished in volume.

"It is so in every country of the world, and the cause is
easy to assign. A certain quantity of water, very small, it
is true, in proportion to the whole, but not negligable, percolates through the soil, either below the sea bottoms by
crevices, fissures and openings due to submarine eruptions,
or on the dry land; for not all the rain water falls upon
impermeable soil. In general, that which is not evapo-
rated, returns to the sea by springs, rivulets, streams and
rivers; but for this there must be a bed of clay, over
which it may follow the slopes. Wherever this impermeable soil is lacking, it continues its descent by infiltra-

tion and saturates the rocks below. This is the water encountered in quarries.

"This water is lost to general circulation. It enters into chemical combination and constitutes the hydrates. If it penetrates far enough, it attains a temperature sufficient for its transformation into steam, and such is generally the origin of volcanoes and earthquakes. But, within the soil, as in the open air, a sensible proportion of the water in circulation becomes changed into hydrates, and even into oxides ; there is nothing like humidity for the rapid formation of rust. Thus recombined, the elements of water, hydrogen and oxygen, disappear as water. Thermal waters also constitute another interior system of circulation ; they are derived from the surface, but they do not return there, nor to the sea. The surface water of the earth, either by entering into new combinations, or by penetrating the lower rock-strata, is diminishing, and it will diminish more and more as the earth's heat is dissipated. The heat-wells which have been dug within a hundred years, in the neighborhood of the principal cities of the world, and which afford the heat necessary for domestic purposes, will become exhausted as the internal temperature diminishes. The day will come when the earth will be cold to its center, and that day will be coincident with an almost total disappearance of water.

"For that matter, gentlemen, this is likely to be the fate of several bodies in our solar system. Our neighbor the

NO MORE WATER.

moon, whose volume and mass are far inferior to those of the earth, has grown cold more rapidly, and has traversed more quickly the phases of its astral life; its ancient ocean-beds, on which we, today, recognize the indubitable traces of water action, are entirely dry; there is no evidence of any kind of evaporation; no cloud has been discovered, and the spectroscope reveals no indication of the presence of the vapor of water. On the other hand, the planet Mars, also smaller than the earth, has beyond a doubt reached a more advanced phase of development, and is known not to possess a single body of water worthy of the name of ocean, but only inland seas of medium extent and slight depth, united with each other by canals. That there is less water on Mars than on the earth is a fact proved by observation; clouds are far less numerous, the atmosphere is much dryer, evaporation and condensation take place with greater rapidity, and the polar snows show variations, depending upon the season, much more extensive than those which take place upon the earth. Again, the planet Venus, younger than the earth, is surrounded by an immense atmosphere, constantly filled with clouds. As for the large planet Jupiter, we can only make out, as it were, an immense accumulation of vapors. Thus, the four worlds of which we know the most, confirm, each in its own way, the theory of a secular decrease in the amount of the earth's water.

" I am very happy to say in this connection that the theory of a general levelling process, maintained by my learned colleague, is confirmed by the present condition of the planet Mars. That eminent geologist told us a few moments ago, that, owing to the continuous action of rivers, plains almost horizontal would constitute the final form of the earth's surface. That is what has already happened in the case of Mars. The beaches near the sea are so flat that they are easily and frequently inundated, as every one knows. From season to season hundreds of thousands of square kilometers are alternately exposed or covered by a thin layer of water. This is notably the case on the western shores of the Kaiser sea. On the moon this levelling process has not taken place. There was not time enough for it; before its consummation, the air, the wind and the water had vanished.

" It is then certain that, while the earth is destined to

undergo a process of levelling, as my eminent colleague has so clearly explained, it will at the same time gradually lose the water which it now possesses.   To all appearances, the latter process is now going on more rapidly than the former.   As the earth loses its internal heat and becomes cold, crevasses will undoubtedly form, as in the case of the moon.   The complete extinction of terrestrial heat will result in contractions, in the formation of hollow spaces below the surface, and the contents of the ocean will flow into these hollows, without being changed into vapor, and will be either absorbed or combined with the metallic rocks, in the form of ferric hydrates.   The amount of water will thus go on diminishing indefinitely, and finally totally disappear.   Plants, deprived of their essential constituent, will become transformed, but must at last perish.

" The animal species will also become modified, but there will always be herbivora and carnivora, and the extinction of the former will involve, inevitably, that of the latter ; and at last, the human race itself, notwithstanding its power of adaption, will die of hunger and of thirst, on the bosom of a dried-up world.

" I conclude, therefore, gentlemen, that the end of the world will not be brought about by a new deluge, but by the loss of its water.   Without water terrestrial life is impossible ; water constitutes the chief constituent of every living thing.   It is present in the human body in the enormous proportion of seventy per cent. Without it, neither plants nor animals can exist. Either as a liquid, or in a state of vapor, it is the condition of life. Its suppression would be the death-warrant of humanity, and this death-warrant nature will serve upon us a dozen million years hence. I will add that this will take place before the completion of the erosion explained by the president of the geological society of France; for he, himself, was careful to note that the period of 4,000,000 years was dependent upon the hypothesis that the causes now in operation continued to act as they do today; and, furthermore, he, himself, admits that the manifestations of internal energy cannot immediately cease. Upheavals, at various points, will occur for a long period, and the growth of the land area from such causes as the formation of deltas, and volcanic and coral islands, will still go on for some time. The period which he indicated, therefore, represents only the minimum."

Such was the address of the permanent secretary of the academy of meteorology. The audience had listened with the deepest attention to both speakers, and it was evident, from its bearing, that it was fully reassured concerning the fate of the world; it seemed even to have altogether forgotten the existence of the comet.

"The president of the physical society of France has the floor."

At this invitation, a young woman, elegantly dressed

7

THE LADY PRESIDENT OF THE PHYSICAL SOCIETY ADDRESSING THE INSTITUTE.

in the most perfect taste, ascended the tribune.

"My two learned colleagues," she began, without further preamble, "are both right; for, on the one hand, it is impossible to deny that meteorological agents, with the assistance of gravity, are working insensibly to level the world, whose crust is ever thickening and solidifying; and, on the other hand, the amount of water on the surface of our planet is decreasing from century to century. These two facts may be considered as scientifically established. But, gentlemen, it does not seem to me that the end of the world will be due to either the submergence of the continents, or to an insufficient supply of water for plant and animal life."

This new declaration, this announcement of a third hypothesis, produced in the audience an astonishment bordering upon stupor.

"Nor do I believe," the graceful orator hastened to add, "that the final catastrophe can be set down to the comet, for I agree with my two eminent predecessors, that worlds do not die by accident, but of old age.

"Yes, doubtless, gentlemen," she continued, "the water will grow less, and, perhaps, in the end totally disappear; yet, it is not this lack of water which in itself will bring about the end of things, but its climatic consequences. The decrease in the amount of aqueous vapor in the atmosphere will lead to a general lowering of the temperature, and humanity will perish *with cold.*

"I need inform no one here that the atmosphere we breathe is composed of seventy-nine per cent. of nitrogen and twenty per cent. of oxygen, and that of the remaining one per cent. about one-half is aqueous vapor and three ten-thousandths is carbonic acid, the remainder being ozone, or electrified oxygen, ammonia, hydrogen and a few other gases, in exceedingly small quantities. Nitrogen and oxygen, then, form ninety-nine per cent. of the atmosphere, and the vapor of water one-half the remainder.

"But, gentlemen, from the point of view of vegetable and animal life, this half of one per cent. of aqueous vapor is of supreme importance, and so far as temperature and climate are concerned, I do not hesitate to assert that it is more essential than all the rest of the atmosphere.

"The heat waves, coming from the sun to the earth, which warm the soil and are thence returned and scattered through the atmosphere into space, in their passage through the air meet with the oxygen and nitrogen atoms and with the molecules of aqueous vapor. These molecules are so thinly scattered (for they occupy but the hundredth part of the space occupied by the others), that one might infer that the retention of any heat whatever is due rather to the nitrogen and oxygen than to the aqueous vapor. Indeed, if we consider the atoms alone, we find two hundred oxygen and nitrogen atoms for

one of aqueous vapor. Well, this one atom has eighty times more energy, more effective power to retain
radiant heat, than the two hundred others; consequently,
a molecule of the vapor of water is 16,000 times more
effective than a molecule of dry air, in absorbing and in
radiating heat—for these two properties are reciprocally
proportional.

"To diminish by any great amount the number of these
invisible molecules of the vapor of water, is to immediately render the earth uninhabitable, notwithstanding its
oxygen; even the equatorial and tropical regions will suddenly lose their heat and will be condemned to the cold of
mountain summits covered with perpetual snow and frost:
in place of luxurious plants, of flowers and fruits, of birds
and nests, of the life which swarms in the sea and upon
the land; instead of murmuring brooks and limpid rivers,
of lakes and seas, we shall be surrounded only by ice in
the midst of a vast desert—and when I say *we*, gentlemen,
you understand we shall not linger long as witnesses, for
the very blood would freeze in our veins and arteries, and
every human heart would soon cease to beat. Such would
be the consequences of the suppression of this half hundredth part of aqueous vapor which, disseminated through
the atmosphere, beneficently protects and preserves all
terrestrial life as in a hot-house.

"The principles of thermodynamics prove that the
temperature of space is 273° below zero. And this, gentle-

PRIMARY VEGETATION AT THE NORTH POLE.

men, is the more than glacial cold in which our planet
will sleep when it shall have lost this airy garment in
whose sheltering warmth it is today enwrapped.   Such is
the fate with which the gradual loss of the earth's water
threatens the world, and this death by cold will be

inevitably ours, if our earthly sojourn is long enough.

"This end is all the more certain, because not only the aqueous vapor is diminishing, but also the oxygen and nitrogen, in brief, the entire atmosphere. Little by little the oxygen becomes fixed in the various oxides which are constantly forming on the earth's surface; this is the case also with the nitrogen, which disappears in the soil and vegetation, never wholly regaining a gaseous state; and the atmosphere penetrates by its weight into the land and sea, descending into subterranean depths. Little by little, from century to century, it grows less. Once, as for example in the early primary period, it was of vast extent; the earth was almost wholly covered by water, only the first granite upheavel broke the surface of the universal ocean, and the atmosphere was saturated with a quantity of aqueous vapor immeasurably greater than that it now holds. This is the explanation of the high temperature of those bygone days, when the tropical plants of our time, the tree ferns, such as the calamites, the equisetaceæ, the sigillaria and the lepidodendrons flourished as luxuriously at the poles as at the equator. Today, both the atmosphere and aqueous vapor have considerably diminished in amount. In the future they are destined to disappear. Jupiter, which is still in its primary period, possesses an immense atmosphere full of vapors. The moon does not appear to have any at all, so that the temperature is always below the freezing point, even in the sunlight, and the atmosphere of Mars is sensibly rarer than ours.

"As to the time which must elapse before this reign of cold caused by the diminution of the aqueous atmosphere which surrounds the globe, I also would adopt the period of 10,000,000 years, as estimated by the speaker who preceded me. Such, ladies, are the stages of world-life which nature seems to have marked out, at least for the planetary system to which we belong. I conclude, therefore, that the fate of the earth will be the same as that of the moon, and that when it loses the airy garment which now guarantees it against the loss of the heat received from the sun, it will perish with cold."

At this point the chancellor of the Columbian academy, who had come that very day from Bogota by an elcetric air-ship to participate in the discussion, requested permission to speak. It was known that he had founded on the very equator itself, at an enormous altitude, an observatory overlooking the entire planet, from which one might see both the celestial poles at the same time, and which he had named in honor of a French astronomer who had devoted his whole life to making known his favorite science and to establishing its great philosophical importance. He was received with marked sympathy and attention.

"Gentlemen," he said, on reaching the desk, "in these two sessions we have had an admirable resumé of the curious theories which modern science is in a position to offer us,

upon the various ways in which our world may come to an
end. The burning of the atmosphere, or suffocation caused
by the shock of the rapidly approaching comet; the
submergence of the continents in the far future beneath
the sea; the drying up of the earth as a result of the
gradual loss of its water; and finally, the freezing of our
unhappy planet, grown old as the decaying and frozen
moon. Here, if I mistake not, are five distinct possible
ends.

PERISHING FROM COLD.

"The director of the observatory has announced that he does not believe in the first two, and that in his opinion a collison with the comet will have only insignificant results. I agree with him in every respect, and I now wish to add, after listening attentively to the learned addresses of my distinguished colleagues, that I do not believe in the other three either.

"Ladies," continued the Columbian astronomer, "you know as well as we do that nothing is eternal. In the bosom of nature all is change. The buds of the spring burst into flowers, the flowers in their turn become fruit, the generations succeed each other, and life accomplishes its mission. So the world which we inhabit will have its end as it has had its beginning, but neither the comet, nor water, nor the lack of water are to cause its death agony. To my mind the whole question hangs upon a single word in the closing sentence of the very remarkable address which has just been made by our gracious colleague, the president of the physical society.

"The sun! Yes, here is the key to the whole problem.

"Terrestrial life depends upon its rays. I say depends upon them—life is a form of solar energy. It is the sun which maintains water in a liquid state, and the atmosphere in a gaseous one; without it all would be solid and lifeless; it is the sun which draws water from the sea, the lakes, the rivers, the moist soil; which forms the clouds and sets the air in motion; which produces rain and con-

trols the fruitful circulation of the water ; thanks to the
solar light and heat, the plants assimilate the carbon contained in the carbonic acid of the atmosphere, and in sepa-
rating the oxygen from the carbon and appropriating the
latter the plant performs a great work ; to this conversion
of solar into vital energy, as well as to the shade of the
thick-leaved trees, is due the freshness of the forests ; the
wood which blazes on our hearthstones does but render up
to us its store of solar heat, and when we consume gas or
coal today, we are only setting free the rays imprisoned
millions of years ago in the forests of the primary age.
Electricity itself is but a form of energy whose original
source is the sun.   It is, then, the sun which murmurs in
the brook, which whispers in the wind, which moans in
the tempest, which blossoms in the rose, which trills
in the throat of the nightingale, which gleams in the
lightning, which thunders in the storm, which sings or
wails in the vast symphony of nature.

"Thus the solar heat is changed into air or water
currents, into the expansive force of gases and vapors, into
electricity, into woods, flowers, fruits and muscular energy.
So long as this brilliant star supplies us with sufficient
heat the continuance of the world and of life is assured.

"The probable cause of the heat of the sun is the condensation of the nebula in which this central body of our
system had its origin.   This conversion of mechanical
energy must have produced 28,000,000 degrees centigrade.

You know gentlemen, that a kilogram of coal, falling from an infinite distance to the sun, would produce, by its impact, six thousand times more heat than by its combustion. At the present rate of radiation, this supply of heat accounts for the emission of thermal energy for a period of 22,000,000 years, and it is probable that the sun has been burning far longer, for there is nothing to prove that the elements of the nebula were absolutely cold ; on the contrary they themselves were originally a source of heat. The temperature of this great day-star does not seem to have fallen any ; for its condensation is still going on, and it may make good the loss by radiation. Nevertheless, everything has an end. If at some future stage of condensation the sun's density should equal that of the earth, this condensation would yield a fresh amount of heat sufficient to maintain for 17,000,000 years the same temperature which now sustains terrestrial life, and this period may be prolonged if we admit a diminution in the rate of radiation, a fall of meteorites, or a further condensation resulting in a density greater than that of the earth. But, however far we put off the end, it must come at last. The suns which are extinguished in the heavens, offer so many examples of the fate reserved for our own luminary ; and in certain years such tokens of death are numerous.

" But in that long period of seventeen or twenty million years, or more, who can say what the marvellous power of adaptation, which physiology and paleontology have re-

vealed in every variety of animal and vegetable life, may
not do for humanity, leading it, step by step, to a state of
physical and intellectual perfection as far above ours, as
ours is above that of the ignuanodon, the stegosaurus and
the compsognathus? Who can say that our fossil remains
will not appear to our successors as monstrous as those of
the dinosaurus? Perhaps the stability of temperature of
that future time may make it seem doubtful whether any
really intelligent race could have existed in an epoch subjected, as ours is, to such erratic variations of temperature,
to the capricious changes of weather which characterize
our seasons. And, who knows if before that time some
immense cataclysm, some general change may not bury
the past in new geological strata and inaugurate new periods, quinquennial, sexsennial, differing totally from the
preceding ones?

" One thing is certain, that the sun will finally lose its
heat; it is condensing and contracting, and its fluidity is
decreasing. The time will come when the circulation,
which now supplies the photosphere, and makes the central mass a reservoir of radiant energy, will be obstructed
and will slacken. The radiation of heat and light will
then diminish, and vegetable and animal life will be more
and more restricted to the earth's equatorial regions.
When this circulation shall have ceased, the brilliant photosphere will be replaced by a dark opaque crust which
will prevent all luminous radiation. The sun will become

a dark red ball, then a black one, and night will be perpetual. The moon, which shines only by reflection, will no longer illumine the lonely nights. Our planet will receive no light but that of the stars. The solar heat having vanished, the atmosphere will remain undisturbed, and an absolute calm, unbroken by any breath of air, will reign.

"If the oceans still exist they will be frozen ones, no evaporation will form clouds, no rain will fall, no stream will flow. Perhaps, as has been observed in the case of stars on the eve of extinction, some last flare of the expiring torch, some accidental development of heat, due to the falling in of the sun's crust, will give us back for a while the old-time sun, but this will only be the precursor of the end ; and the earth, a dark ball, a frozen tomb, will continue to revolve about the black sun, travelling through an endless night and hurrying away with all the solar system into the abyss of space. *It is to the extinction of the sun that the earth will owe its death, twenty, perhaps forty million years hence.*"

The speaker ceased, and was about to leave the platform, when the director of the academy of fine arts begged to be heard :

"Gentlemen," he said, from his chair, "if I have understood rightly, the end of the world will in any case result from cold, and only several million years hence. If, then, a painter should endeavor to represent the last day, he

A WORLD OF ICE.

ought to shroud the earth in ice, and cover it with skeletons."

"Not exactly," replied the Columbian chancellor. "It is not cold which produces glaciers,—it is *heat*.

"If the sun did not evaporate the sea water there would be no clouds, and but for the sun there would be no wind. For the formation of glaciers a sun is necessary, to vaporize the water and to transport it in clouds and then to condense it. Every kilogram of vapor formed represents a quantity of solar heat sufficient to raise five kilograms of cast-iron to its fusing point (110°). By lessening the intensity of the sun's action we exhaust the glacier supply.

"So that it is not the snow, nor the glaciers which will cover the earth, but the frozen remnant of the sea. For a long time previously streams and rivers will have ceased to exist and every atmospheric current will have disappeared, unless indeed, before giving up the ghost, the sun shall have passed through one of those spasms to which we referred a moment ago, shall have released the ice from sleep and have produced new clouds and aerial currents, re-awakened the springs, the brooks and the rivers, and after this momentary but deceitful awakening, shall have fallen back again into lethargy. That day will have no morrow."

Another voice, that of a celebrated electrician, was heard from the center of the hemicycle.

"All these theories of death by cold," he observed, "are plausible. But the end of the world by fire? This has been referred to only in connection with the comet. It may happen otherwise.

"Setting aside a possible sinking of the continents into the central fire, brought about by an earthquake on a large scale, or some widespread dislocation of the earth's crust, it seems to me that, without any collision, a superior will might arrest our planet midway in its course and transform its motion into heat."

"A will?" interrupted another voice. "But positive science does not admit the possibility of miracles in nature."

"Nor I, either," replied the electrician. "When I say 'will,' I mean an ideal, invisible force. Let me explain.

"The earth is flying through space with a velocity of 106,000 kilometers per hour, or 29,460 meters per second.

If some star, active or extinct, should emerge from space, so as to form with the sun a sort of electro-dynamic couple with our planet on its axis, acting upon it like a brake— if, in a word, for any reason, the earth should be suddenly arrested in its orbit, its mechanical energy would be changed into molecular motion, and its temperature would be suddenly raised to such a degree as to reduce it entirely to a gaseous state."

" Gentlemen," said the director of the Mont Blanc observatory, from his chair, " the earth might perish by fire in still another manner. We have lately seen in the sky a temporary star which, in a few weeks, passed from the sixteenth to the fourth magnitude. This distant sun had suddenly become 50,000 times hotter and more luminous. If such a fate should overtake our sun, nothing living would be left upon our planet. It is probable, from the study of the spectrum of the light emitted by this burning star, that the cause of this sudden conflagration was the entrance of this sun and its system into some kind of nebula. Our own sun is travelling with a frightful velocity in the direction of the constellation of Hercules, and may very well some day encounter an obstacle of this nature."

" To resume," continued the director of the Paris observatory, " after all we have just now heard, we see that our planet will be at a loss to choose among so many modes of death. I have as little fear now as before of any danger from the present comet. But it must be confessed that, solely from the point of view of the astronomer, this poor, wandering earth is exposed to more than one peril. The child born into this world, and destined to reach the age of maturity, may be compared to a person stationed at the entrance to a narrow street, one of those picturesque streets of the sixteenth century, lined with houses at whose every window is a marksman armed with a good weapon of the latest model. This person must traverse the entire length of the street, without being stricken down by the weapons levelled upon him at close range. Every disease which lies in wait and threatens us, is on hand : dentition, convulsion, croup, meningitis, measles, smallpox, typhoid fever, pneumonia, enteritis, brain fever, heart disease, consumption, diabetes, apoplexy, cholera, influenza, etc., etc., for we omit many, and our hearers will have no difficulty in supplementing this offhand enumeration. Will our unhappy traveller reach the end of the street safe and sound ? If he does, it will only be to die, just the same.

"Thus our planet pursues its way along its heavenly path, with a speed of more than 100,000 kilometers per hour, and, at the same time, the sun hurries it on, with all the planets, toward the constellation of Hercules. Recapitulating what has just been said, and allowing for what may have been omitted : it may meet a comet ten or twenty times larger than itself, composed of deleterious gases which would render the atmosphere irrespirable ; it may encounter a swarm of uranolites, which would have upon it the effect of a charge of shot upon a meadow lark; it may meet in its path an invisible sun, much larger than itself, whose shock would reduce it to vapor; it may encounter a sun which would consume it in the twinkling of an eye, as a furnace would consume an apple thrown into it; it may be caught in a system of electric forces, which would act like a brake upon its eleven motions, and which would either melt it, or set it afire, like a platinum wire in a strong current; it may lose the oxygen which supports life; it may be blown up like the crust over a crater; it may collapse in some great earthquake; its dry

" LIKE A CHARGE OF SHOT UPON A MEADOW LARK."

land may disappear, in a second deluge, more universal than the first; it may, on the contrary, lose all its water, an element essential to its organic life; under the attraction of some passing body, it may be detached from the sun and carried away into the cold of stellar space; it may part, not only with the last vestige of its internal heat, which long since has ceased to have any influence upon its surface, but also with the protecting envelope which maintains the temperature necessary to life; one of these days, when the sun has grown dark and cold, it may be neither lighted, nor warmed, nor fertilized; on the other hand, it may be suddenly scorched by an outburst of heat, analogous to what has been observed in temporary stars; not to speak of many other sources of accidents and mortal peril, whose easy enumeration we leave to the geologists paleontologists, meteorologists, physicists, chemists, biologists, physicians, botanists, and even to the veterinary surgeons, inasmuch as the arrival of an army of invisible microbes, if they be but deadly enough, or a well-established epidemic, would suffice to destroy the human race and the principal animal and vegetable species, without working the least harm to the planet itself, from a strictly astronomical point of view."

Just as the speaker was uttering these last words, a voice, which seemed to come from a distance, fell, as it were, from the ceiling overhead. But a few words of explanation may here perhaps be desirable.

As we have said, the observatories established on the higher mountains of the globe were connected by telephone, with the observatory of Paris, and the sender of the message could be heard at a distance from the receiver, without being obliged to apply any apparatus directly to the ear. The reader doubtless recollects that, at the close of the preceding session, a phonogram from Mt. Gaurisankar stated that a photophonic message, which would be at once deciphered, had been received from the inhabitants of Mars. As the translation of this cipher had not arrived at the opening of the evening session, the bureau of communications had connected the Institute with the observatory by suspending a telephonoscope from the dome of the amphitheater.

The voice from above said :

" The astronomers of the equatorial city of Mars warn the inhabitants of the earth that the comet is moving directly toward the earth with a velocity nearly double that of the orbital velocity of Mars. Mechanical motion to be transformed into heat, and heat into electrical energy. Terrible magnetic storms. Move away from Italy."

The voice ceased amid general silence and consternation. There were, however, a few sceptics left, one of whom, editor of La Libre Critique, raising his monocle to his right eye, had risen from the reporters desk and had exclaimed in a penetrating voice :

" I am afraid that the venerable doctors of the Institute

are the victims of a huge joke. No one can ever persuade me that the inhabitants of Mars—admitting that there are any and they have really sent us a warning—know Italy by name. I doubt very much if one of them ever heard of the Commentaries of Cæsar or the History of the Popes, especially as "—

The orator, who was launching into an interesting dithyrambus, was at this point suddenly squelched by the turning off of the electric lights. With the exception of the illuminated square in the ceiling, the room was plunged in darkness and the voice added these six words: "This is the despatch from Mars;" and thereupon the following symbols appeared on the plate of the telephonoscope:

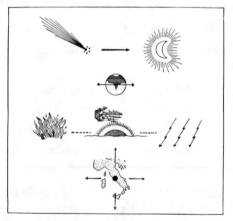

As this picture could only be seen by holding the head in a very fatiguing position, the president touched a bell and an assistant appeared, who by means of a projector and mirror transferred these hieroglyphics to a screen on the wall behind the desk, so that every one could readily see and analyze them at their leisure. Their interpretation was easy; nothing indeed could be more simple. The figure representing the comet needed no explanation. The arrow indicates the motion of the comet towards a heavenly body, which as seen from Mars presents phases, and sparkles like a star; this means the earth, naturally so delineated by the Martians, for their eyes, developed in a medium less luminous than ours, are somewhat more sensitive and distinguish the phases of the Earth, and this the more readily because their atmosphere is rarer and more transparent. (For us the phases of Venus are just on the limit of visibility.) The double globe represents Mars looking at the Kaiser sea, the most characteristic feature of Martian geography, and indicates a velocity for the comet double the orbital velocity, or a little less, for the line does not quite reach the edge. The flames indicate the transformation of motion into heat; the aurora borealis and the lightning which follow, the transformation into electric and magnetic force. Finally, we recognize the boot of Italy, visible from Mars, and the black spot marks the locality threatened, according to their calculation, by one of the most dangerous fragments of the head of the comet; while the four arrows radiating in the direction of the four cardinal points of the compass seem to counsel removal from the point menaced.

The photophonic message from the Martians was much longer and far more complicated. The astronomers on Mt. Gaurisankar had previously received several such, and had discovered that they were sent from a very important, intellectual and scientific center situated in the equatorial zone not far from Meridian bay. The last message, whose general meaning is given above, was the most important. The remainder of it had not been transmitted, as it was obscure and it was not certain that its exact meaning had been made out.

The president rang his bell for order. He was about to sum up what had been said, before adjourning the meeting.

"Gentlemen," he began, "although it is after midnight, it will be of interest, before we separate, to summarize what has been told us in these two solemn sessions.

"The last despatch from Gaurisankar may well impress you. It seems clear that the inhabitants of Mars are farther advanced in science than ourselves, and this is not surprising, for they are a far older race and have had centuries innumerable in which to achieve this progress. Moreover, they may be much more highly organized than we are, they may possess better eyes, instruments of greater perfection, and intellectual faculties of a higher order. We observe, too, that their calculations, while in accord with ours as to the collision, are more precise, for they designate the very point which is to receive the greatest shock. The advice to flee from Italy should therefore be followed, and I shall at once telephone the Pope, who at this very moment is assembling the prelates of entire Christendom.

" So the comet will collide with the earth, and no one can yet foresee the consequences. But in all probability the disturbance will be local and the world will not be destroyed. The carbonic-oxide is not likely to penetrate the respirable portions of the atmosphere, but there will be an enormous development of heat.

" As to the veritable end of the world, of all the hypotheses which today permit us to forecast that event the most probable is the last—that explained to us by the learned chancellor of the Columbian academy : the life of the planet depends upon the sun ; so long as the sun shines humanity is safe, unless indeed the diminution of the atmosphere and aqueous vapor should usher in before that time the reign of cold. In the former case we have yet before us twenty million years of life ; in the latter only ten.

" Let us then await the night of July 13-14 without despair. I advise those who can to pass these fête days in Chicago, or better still in San Francisco, Honolulu or Noumea. The trans-Atlantic electric air-ships are so numerous· and well managed that millions of travellers may make the journey before Saturday night."

THE LAST JUDGMENT.
(From the ceiling of the Sistine Chapel.)

CHAPTER V.

WHILE the above scientific discussions were taking place at Paris, meetings of a similar character were being held at London, Chicago, St. Petersburg, Yokohama, Melbourne, New York, and in all the principal cities of the world, in which every effort was made to throw light upon the great problem which so universally preoccupied the attention of humanity. At Oxford a theological council of the Reformed church was convened, in which religious traditions and interpretations were discussed at great length. To recite, or even to summarize here the proceedings of all these congresses would be an endless task, but we cannot omit reference to that of the Vatican as the most important from a religious point of view, just as that of the Institute of Paris was from a scientific one.

The council had been divided into a certain number of sections or committees, and the then often discussed question of the end of the world had been referred to one of these committees. Our duty here is to reproduce as accurately as possible the physiognomy of the main session, devoted to the discussion of this problem.

The patriarch of Jerusalem, a man of great piety and profound faith, was the first to speak in Latin. "Venerable fathers," he began, "I cannot do better than to open before you the Holy Gospel. Permit me to quote literally." He then read the words of the evangelists* describing the last days of the earth, and went on :

" These words are taken verbatim from the Gospels, and you know that on this point the evangelists are in perfect accord.

" You also know, most reverend fathers, that the last great day is pictured in still more striking language in the

---

*St. Matthew, xxiv. and xvi.; St. Mark, xiii.; St. Luke, xvii. and xxi.

THE PATRIARCH OF JERUSALEM ADDRESSING THE COUNCIL.

Apocalypse of St. John. But every word of the Scriptures is known to you, and, in the presence of so learned an audience, it seems to me superfluous, if not out of place, to make further citations from what is upon every lip."

Such was the beginning of the address of the patriarch of Jerusalem. His remarks were divided under three heads : First, the teachings of Christ ; second, the traditions of the Church ; third, the dogma of the resurrection of the body, and of the last judgment. Taking first the form of an historical statement, the address soon became a sort of sermon, of vast range ; and when the orator, passing from St. Paul to Clement of Alexandria, Tertulian and Origen, reached the council of Nice and the dogma of universal resurrection, he was carried away by his subject in such a flight of eloquence as to move the heart of every prelate before him. Several, who had renounced the apostolic faith of the earlier centuries, felt themselves again under its spell. It must be said that the surroundings lent themselves marvellously to the occasion. The assembly took place in the Sistine chapel. The immense and imposing painting of Michael Angelo, like a new apocalyptic heaven, was before every eye. The awful mingling of bodies, arms and legs, so forcibly and strangely foreshortened ; Christ, the judge of the world ; the damned borne struggling away by hideous devils ; the dead issuing from their tombs ; the skeletons returning to life and reclothing themselves with flesh ; the frightful

terror of humanity trembling in the presence of the wrath
of God—all seemed to give a vividness, a reality, to the
magnificent periods of the patriarch's oratory, and at times,
in certain effects of light, one might almost hear the advancing trumpet sounding from heaven the call of judgment, and see between earth and sky the moving hosts
of the resurrection.

Scarcely had the patriarch of Jerusalem finished his
speech, when an independent bishop, one of the most
ardent dissenters of the council, the learned Mayerstross,

MAYERSTROSS.

rushed to the tribune, and
began to insist that nothing in the Gospel, or the
traditions of the Church,
should be taken literally.

"The letter kills," he
cried, "the spirit vivifies!
Everything is subject to the
law of progress and change.
The world moves.   En-
lightened Christians cannot
any longer admit the resurrection of the body.   All
these images," he added,
"were good for the days of
the catacombs.   For a long
time no one has believed in

them. Such ideas are opposed to science, and, most reverend fathers you know, as well as I do, that we must be
in accord with science, which has ceased to be, as in the
time of Galileo, the humble servant of theology : theo-
logiæ humilis ancilla.

" The body cannot be reconstituted, even by a miracle, so
long as its molecules return to nature and are appropriated,
successively, by so many beings—human, animal and
vegetable. We are formed of the dust of the dead, and,
in the future, the molecules of oxygen, hydrogen, nitrogen,
carbon, phosphorus, sulphur, or iron, which make up our
flesh and our bones, will be incorporated in other human
organisms. This change is perpetual, even during life.
One human being dies every second ; that is more than
86,000 each day, more than 30,000,000 each year, more
than three milliards each century. In a hundred centuries
—not a long period in the history of a planet, the number
of the resurrected would be three hundred milliards. If
the human race lived but a 100,000 years—and no one
here is ignorant of the fact that geological and astronomical periods are estimated by millions of years—there
would be gathered before the judgment throne something
like three thousand milliards of men, women and children.
My estimate is a modest one, because I take no account of
the secular increase in population. You may reply to me,
that only the saved will rise ! What, then, will become
of the others ? Two weights and two measures ! Death

and life ! Night and day, good and evil ! Divine injus-
tice and good-will, reigning together over creation ! But,
no, you will not accept such a solution. The eternal law
is the same for all. Well ! What will you do with these
thousands of milliards ? Show me the valley of Jehosha-
phat vast enough to contain them. Will you spread them
over the surface of the globe, do away with the oceans and
the icefields of the poles, and cover the world with a forest
of human bodies ? So be it ! And afterwards ? What
will become of this immense host ? No, most holy
fathers, our beliefs must not, cannot, be taken literally.
Would that there were here no theologians with closed
eyes, that look only within, but astronomers with open
eyes, that look without."

These words had been uttered in the midst of an
indescribable tumult ; several times they wished to silence
the Croatian bishop, gesticulating violently and denounc-
ing him as schismatic ; but the rules did not permit this,
for the greatest liberty was allowed in the discussion. An
Irish cardinal called down upon him the thunders of the
Church, and spoke of excommunication and anathema ;
then, a distinguished prelate of the Gallican church, no less
a person than the archbishop of Paris himself, ascended the
rostrum and declared that the dogma of the resurrection
of the dead might be discussed without incurring any
canonical blame, and that it might be interpreted in entire
harmony with reason and faith. According to him one

might admit the dogma, and at the same time recognize the rational impossibility of a resurrection of the body !

"The Doctor Angelicus," he said, speaking of St. Thomas, "maintained that the complete dissolution of every human body by fire would take place before the resurrection. (Summa theologica, III.) I readily concede with Calmet (on the resurrection of the dead) that to the omnipotence of the Creator it would not be impossible to reassemble the scattered molecules in such a way that the resurrected body should not contain a single one which did not belong to it at some time during its mortal life. But such a miracle is not necessary. St. Thomas has himself shown (loco citato) that this complete material identity is by no means indispensable to establish the perfect identity of the resurrected body with the body destroyed by death. I also think, therefore, that the letter should give way to the spirit.

"What is the principle of identity in a living body ? Assuredly it does not consist in the complete and persistent identity of its *matter*. For in this continual change and renewal, which is the very essence of physiological life, the elements, which have belonged successively from infancy to old age to the same human being, would form a colossal body. In this torrent of life the elements pass and change ceaselessly ; but the organism remains the same, notwithstanding the modifications in its size, its form and its constitution. Does the growing stem of the oak,

9

hidden between its two cotyledons, cease to be the same plant when it has become a mighty oak? Is the embryo of the caterpillar, while yet in the egg, no longer the same insect when it becomes a caterpillar, and then a chrysalis, and then a butterfly? Is individuality lost as the child passes through manhood to old age? Assuredly not. But in the case of the oak, the butterfly, and the man, is there a single remaining molecule of those which constituted the growing stem of the oak, the egg of the caterpillar or the human embryo? What then is the principle which persists through all these changes? This principle is a reality, not a fiction. It is not the soul, for the plants have life, and yet no souls, in the meaning of the word as we use it. Nevertheless, it must be an imponderable agent. Does it survive the body? It is possible. St. Gregory of Nyssus believed so. If it remains united to the soul, it may be invoked to furnish it with a new body identical with that which death has destroyed, even though this body should not possess *a single molecule* which it possessed at any period of its terrestrial life, and this would be as truly our body as that which we had when five, fifteen, or thirty, or sixty years of age.

" Such a conception agrees perfectly with the expressions of holy writ, according to which it is certain that after a period of separation the soul will again take on the body forever.

" In addition to St. Gregory of Nyssus, permit me, most

reverend fathers, to cite a philosopher Leibnitz, who held the opinion that the physiological principle of life was imponderable but not incorporeal, and that the soul remains united to this principle, although separated from the ponderable and visible body. I do not pretend to either accept or reject this hypothesis. I only note that it may serve to explain the dogma of the resurrection, in which every Christian should firmly believe."

"This effort to conciliate reason and faith," interrupted the Croatian bishop, "is worthy of praise, but it seems to me more ingenious than probable. Are these bodies, bodies like our own? If they are perfect, incorruptible, fitted to their new conditions, they must not possess any organ for which there is no use. Why a mouth, if they do not eat? Why legs, if they do not walk? Why arms, if they do not work? One of the fathers of the early church, Origen, whose personal sacrifice is not forgotten, thought these bodies must be perfect spheres. That would be logical but not very beautiful or interesting."

"It is better to admit with St. Gregory of Nyssus and St. Augustin," replied the archbishop, "that the resurrected body will have the human form, a transparent veil of the beauty of the soul."

Thus was the modern theory of the Church on the resurrection of the body summed up by the French cardinal. As to the objections on the score of the locality of the resurrection, the number of the resurrected, the insufficiency of surface on the globe, the final abode of the elect and the damned, it was impossible to come to any common understanding for the contradictions were irreconcilable. The resultant impression was, however, that these matters also should be understood figuratively, that neither the heaven or the hell of the theologian represented any definite place, but rather states of the soul, of happiness or of misery, and that life, whatever its form, would be perpetuated on the countless worlds which people infinite space. And so it appeared that Christian thought had gradually become transformed, among the enlightened, and followed the progress of astronomy and the other sciences.

The council had been held on Tuesday evening, that is to say on the day following the two meetings of the Institute, of which an account has been given above. The Pope had made public the advice of the president of the Institute to leave Italy on the fatal day, but no attention had been paid to it, partly because death is a deliverance for every believer, and partly because most theologians denied the existence even of inhabitants upon Mars.

CHAPTER VI.

It is now time to pause, amid the eventful scenes through which we are passing, in order to consider this new fear of the end of the world with others which have preceded it, and to pass rapidly in review the remarkable history of this idea, which has reappeared again and again in the past. At the time of which we are speaking, this subject was the sole theme of conversation in every land and in every tongue.

133

As to the dogma "Credo Resurrectionem Carnis," the addresses of the fathers of the Church before the council assembled in the Sistine chapel at Rome, were, on the whole, in accord with the opinion expressed by the cardinal archbishop of Paris. The clause "et vitam æternam" was tacitly ignored, in view of the possible discoveries of astronomy and psychology. These addresses epitomized, as it were, the history of the doctrine of the end of the world as held by the Christian Church in all ages.

This history is interesting, for it is also the history of the human mind face to face with its own destiny, and we believe it of sufficient importance to devote to it a separate chapter. For the time being, therefore, we abandon our role as the chronicler of the twenty-fourth century, and return to our own times, in order to consider this doctrine from an historical point of view.

The existence of a profound and tenacious faith is as old as the centuries, and it is a notable fact that all religions, irrespective of Christian dogma, have opened the same door from this mortal life upon the unknown which lies beyond, it is the door of the Divine Comedy of Dante, although the conceptions of paradise, hell and purgatory peculiar to the Christian Church, are not universal.

Zoroaster and the Zend-Avesta taught that the world would perish by fire. The same idea is found in the Epistle of St. Peter. It seems that the traditions of Noah and of Deucalion, according to which the first great disaster to humanity came by flood, indicated that the second great disaster would be of an exactly opposite character.

The apostles Peter and Paul died, probably, in the year 64, during the horrible slaughter ordered by Nero after the burning of Rome, which had been fired at his command and whose destruction he attributed to the Christians in order that he might have a pretext for new persecutions. St. John wrote the Apocalypse in the year 69. The reign of Nero was a bloody one, and martyrdom seemed to be the natural consequence of a virtuous life. Prodigies appeared on every hand ; there were comets, falling stars, eclipses, showers of blood, monsters, earthquakes, famines, pestilences, and above all, there was the Jewish war and the destruction of Jerusalem. Never, perhaps, were so many horrors, so much cruelty and madness, so many catastrophes, crowded into so short a period as in the years 64-69 A.D. The little church of Christ was apparently dispersed. It was impossible to remain in Jerusalem. The horrors of the reign of terror of 1793, and of the Commune of 1871, were as nothing in comparison with those of the Jewish civil war. The family of Jesus was obliged to leave the holy city and to seek safety in flight. False prophets appeared, thus verifying former prophecies. Vesuvius was preparing the terrible eruption of the year 79, and already, in 63, Pompeii had been destroyed by an earthquake.

There was every indication that the end of the world

was at hand.   Nothing was wanting.   The Apocalypse announced it.

But a calm followed the storm.   The terrible Jewish war came to an end ; Nero fell before Galba ; under Vespasian and Titus, peace (71) succeeded war, and—the end of the world was not yet.

Once more it became necessary to interpret anew the words of the evangelists.   The coming of Christ was put off until after the fall of the Roman empire, and thus considerable margin was given to the commentator.   A firm belief in a final and even an imminent catastrophe persisted, but it was couched in vague terms, which robbed the spirit as well as the letter of the prophecy of all precision.   Still, the conviction remained.

St. Augustine devotes the xxth book of the City of God (426) to the regeneration of the world, the resurrection, the last judgment, and the New Jerusalem ; in the xxist book he describes the everlasting torments of hell-fire.   A witness to the fall of Rome and the empire, the bishop of Carthage believed these events to be the first act of the drama.   But the reign of God was to continue a thousand years before the coming of Satan.

St. Gregory, bishop of Tours (573), the first historian of the Franks, began his history as follows : " As I am about to relate the wars of the kings with hostile nations, I feel impelled to declare my belief.   The terror with which men await the end of the world decides me to chronicle the years already passed, that thus one may know exactly how many have elapsed since the beginning of the world."

This tradition was perpetuated from year to year and from century to century, notwithstanding that nature failed to confirm it. Every catastrophe, earthquake, epidemic, famine and flood, every phenomenon, eclipse, comet, storm, sudden darkness and tempest, was looked upon as the forerunner and herald of the final cataclysm. Trembling like leaves in the blast, the faithful awaited the coming judgment; and preachers successfully worked upon this dread apprehension, so deeply rooted in every heart.

But, as generation after generation passed, it became necessary to define again the wide-spread tradition, and about this time the idea of a millennium took form in the minds of commentators. There were many sects which believed that Christ would reign with the saints a thousand years before the day of judgment. St. Irenus, St. Papias, and St. Sulpicius Severus shared this belief, which acquired an exaggerated and sensual form in the minds of many, who looked forward to a day of general rejoicing for the elect and a reign of pleasure. St. Jerome and St. Augustine did much to discredit these views, but did not attack the central doctrine of a resurrection. Commentators on the Apocalypse continued to flourish through the somber night of the middle ages, and in the tenth century especially the belief gained ground that the year 1000 was to usher in the great change.

This conviction of an approaching end of the world, if not universal, was at least very general. Several charters of the period began with this sentence : Termino mundi appropinquante: "The end of the world drawing near." In spite of some exceptions, it seems difficult not to share the opinion of historians, notably of Michelet, Henry Martin, Guizot, and Duruy, regarding the prevalence of this belief throughout Christendom. Doubtless, neither the French monk Gerbert, at that time Pope Sylvester II., nor King Robert of France, regulated their lives by their superstition, but it had none the less penetrated the conscience of the faint-hearted, and many a sermon was preached from this text of the Apocalypse :

VICTIMS OF THE PLAGUE.

"And when the thousand years are expired, Satan shall be loosed out of his prison, and shall go out to deceive the nations which are in the four quarters of the earth . . . and another book was opened, which is the Book of Life . . . and the sea gave up the dead which were in it: and death and hell gave up the dead which were in them : and they were judged every man according to his works . . . and I saw a new heaven and a new earth."

Bernard, a hermit of Thuringia, had taken these very words of Revelation as the text of his preaching, and in about the year 960 he publicly announced that the end of the world was at hand. He even fixed the fatal day itself, as that on which "The Annunciation" and Holy Friday should fall on the same day, a coincidence which really occurred in 992.

Druthmar, a monk of Corbie, prophesied the end of the world for the 24th of March in the year 1000. In many cities popular terror was so great on that day that the people sought refuge in the churches, remaining until midnight, prostrate before the relics of the saints, in order to await there the last trump and to die at the foot of the cross.

From this epoch date many gifts to the Church. Lands and goods were given to the monasteries. Indeed, an authentic and very curious document is preserved, written in the year 1000 by a certain monk, Raoul Glaber, on whose first pages we find : " Satan will soon be unloosed, as prophesied by St. John, *the thousand years having been accomplished.* It is of these years that we are to speak."

The end of the tenth century and the beginning of the eleventh century was a truly strange and fearful period. From 980 to 1040 it seemed as if the angel of death had spread his wings over the world. Famine and pestilence desolated the length and breadth of Europe. There was in the first place the "mal des ardents," the flesh of its victims decaying and falling from the bones, was consumed as by fire, and the members themselves were destroyed and fell away. Wretches thus afflicted thronged the roads leading to the shrines and besieged the churches, filling them with terrible odors, and dying before the relics of the saints. The fearful pest made more than forty thousand victims in Acquitania, and devastated the southern portions of France.

Then came famine, ravaging a large part of Christendom. Of the seventy-three years between 987 and 1060, forty-eight were years of famine and pestilence. The invasion of the Huns, between 910 and 945, revived the horrors of Attila, and the soil was so laid waste by wars between domains and provinces that it ceased to be cultivated. For three years rain fell continuously; it was impossible either to sow or to reap. The earth became barren and was abandoned. "The price of a 'muid' of wheat," writes Raoul Glaber, "rose to sixty gold sous; the rich waxed thin and pale; the poor gnawed the roots of trees, and many were in such extremity as to devour human flesh. The strong fell upon the weak in the public highways, tore them in pieces, and roasted them for food. Children were enticed by an egg or some fruit into byways, where they were devoured. This frenzy of hunger

THE HUT IN THE FOREST OF MÂCON.

was such that the beast was safer than man. Famished children killed their parents, and mothers feasted upon their children. One person exposed human flesh for sale in the market place of Tournus, as if it were a staple article of food. He did not deny the fact and was burned at the stake. Another, stealing this flesh by night from the spot where it had been buried, was also burned alive."

This testimony is that of one who lived at the time and in many cases was an eye witness to what he relates. On every side people were perishing of hunger, and did not scruple to eat reptiles, unclean animals, and even human flesh. In the depths of the forest of Mâcon, in the vicinity of a church dedicated to St. John, a wretch had built a hut in which he strangled pilgrims and wayfarers. One day a traveller entering the hut with his wife to seek rest, saw in a corner the heads of men, women and children. Attempting to fly, they were prevented by their host. They succeeded, however, in escaping, and on reaching Mâcon, related what they had seen. Soldiers were sent to the bloody spot, where they counted forty-eight human heads. The murderer was dragged to the town and burned alive. The hut and the ashes of the funeral pile were seen by Raoul Glaber. So numerous were the corpses that burial was impossible, and disease followed close upon famine. Hordes of wolves preyed upon the unburied. Never before had such misery been known.

War and pillage were the universal rule, but these

scourges from heaven made men somewhat more reason-
able. The bishops came together, and it was agreed to
establish a truce for four days of each week, from Wednesday night to Monday morning. This was known as the
truce of God.

It is not strange that the end of so miserable a world
was both the hope and the terror of this mournful period.

The year 1000, however, passed like its predecessors,
and the world continued to exist. Were the prophets
wrong again, or did the thousand years of Christendom
point to the year 1033? The world waited and hoped.
In that very year occurred a total eclipse of the sun; " The

" BANDS OF WOLVES PREYED UPON THE UNBURIED."

great source of light became saffron colored ; gazing into each others faces men saw that they were pale as death ; every object presented a livid appearance ; stupor seized upon every heart and a general catastrophe was expected." But the end of the world was not yet.

It was to this critical period that we owe the construction of the magnificent cathedrals which have survived the ravages of time and excited the wonder of centuries. Immense wealth had been lavished upon the clergy, and their riches increased by donations and inheritence. A new era seemed to be at hand. " After the year 1000," continues Raoul Glaber, " the holy basilicas throughout the world were entirely renovated, especially in Italy and Gaul, although for the most part they were in no need of repair. Christian nations vied with each other in the erection of magnificent churches. It seemed as if the entire world, animated by a common impulse, shook off the rags of the past to put on a new garment ; and the faithful were not content to rebuild nearly all the episcopal churches, but also embellished the monasteries dedicated to the various saints, and even the chapels in the smaller villages."

The somber year 1000 had followed the vanished centuries into the past, but through what troubled times the Church had passed ! The popes were the puppets of the rival Saxon emperors and the princes of Latium. All Christendom was in arms. The crisis had passed, but the problem of the end of the world remained, and credence in this dread event, though un- certain and vague, was fostered by that profound be- lief in the devil and in prodigies which was yet to endure for centur- ies in the popular mind. The final scene of the last judgment was sculptured o v e r the portals of ev- ery cathedral, and on entering the sanctuary of the church one passed under the balance

of the archangel, on whose left writhed the bodies of the devils and the damned, delivered over to the eternal flames of hell.

But the idea that the world was to end was not confined to the Church. In the twelfth century astrologers terrified Europe by the announcement of a conjunction of all the planets in the constellation of the scales. This conjunction indeed, occurred, for on September 15th all the planets were found between the 180th and 190th degrees of longitude. But the end of the world did not come.

The celebrated alchemist, Arnauld de Villeneuve, foretold it again for the year 1335. In 1406, under Charles VI., an eclipse of the sun, occurring on June 16th, produced a general panic, which is chronicled by Juvénal of the Ursuline Order: "It is a pitiable sight," he says, "to see people taking refuge in the churches as if the world were

about to perish." In 1491 St. Vincent Ferrier wrote a
treatise entitled, " De la Fin du Monde et de la Science
Spirituelle." He allows Christendom as many years of life
as there are verses in the psalter, namely, 2537. Then a
German astrologer, one Stoffler, predicted that on February
20, 1524, a general deluge would result from a conjunction
of the planets. He was very generally believed, and the
panic was extreme. Property situated in valleys, along
river banks, or near the sea, was sold to the less credulous
for a mere nothing. A certain doctor, Auriol, of Toulouse,
had an ark built for himself, his family and his friends,
and Bodin asserts that he was not the only one who took
this precaution.

There were few sceptics. The grand chancellor of
Charles v. sought the advice of Pierre Martyr, who
told him that the event would not be as fatal as was
feared, but that the conjunction of the planets would
doubtless occasion grave disasters. The fatal day ar-

rived . . . and never
had the month of February
been so dry! But this did
not prevent new predic-
tions for the year 1532, by
the astrologer of the elec-
tor of Brandenburg, Jean
Carion ; and again for the
year 1584, by the astrol-

oger Cyprian Lëowitz. It was again a question of a deluge, due to planetary conjunctions. " The terror of the populace," writes a contemporary, Louis Guyon, " was extreme, and the churches could not hold the multitudes which fled to them for refuge ; many made their wills without stopping to think that this availed little if the world was really to perish ; others donated their goods to the clergy, in the hope that their prayers would put off the day of judgment."

In 1588 there was another astrological prediction, couched in apocalyptic language, as follows : " The eighth year following the fifteen hundred and eightieth anniversary of the birth of Christ will be a year of prodigies and terror. If in this terrible year the globe be not dissolved in dust, and the land and the sea be not destroyed, every kingdom will be overthrown and humanity will travail in pain."

As might be expected, the celebrated soothsayer, Nostradamus, is found among these prophets of evil. In his book of rhymed prophecies, entitled Centuries, we find the following quatrain, which excited much speculation :

Quand Georges Dieu crucifiera,
Que Marc le ressuscitera,
Et que St. Jean le portera,
La fin du monde arrivera.

The meaning of which is, that when Easter falls on the twenty-fifth of April (St. Mark's day), Holy Friday will fall on the twenty-third (St. George's day), and Corpus Christi on the twenty-fourth of June (St. John's day), and the end of the world will come. This verse was not without malice, for at this time (Nostradamus died in 1556) the calendar had not been reformed; this was not done until 1582, and it was impossible for Easter to fall on the twenty-fifth of April. In the sixteenth century, the twenty-fifth of April corresponded to the fifteenth; the day following November 4, 1582, was called the fifteenth. After the introduction of the Gregorian calendar, Easter might fall on the twenty-fifth of April, its latest possible date, and this was the case in 1666, 1734, 1886, as it will be again in 1942, 2038, 2190, etc., the end of the world, however, not being a necessary consequence of this coincidence.

Planetary conjunctions, eclipses and comets were alike the basis for prophecies of evil. Among the comets recorded in history we may mention, as the most remarkable from this point of view, that of William the Conqueror, which appeared in 1066, and which is pictured on the tapestry of Queen Matilda, at Bayeux; that of 1264, which,

it is said, disappeared the
very day of the death of
Pope Urban IV.; that of
1327, one of the largest
and most imposing ever
seen, which "presaged"
the death of Frederick,
king of Sicily; that of
1399, which Juvénal, the
Ursuline, described as
"the, harbinger of com-

ing evil;" that of 1402, to which was ascribed the death of
Gian Galeazzo, Visconti, duke of Milan; that of 1456, which
filled all Christendom with terror, under Pope Calixtus
III., during the war with the Turks, and which is associated with the history of the Angelus; and that of 1472,
which preceded the death of the brother of Louis XI.
There were others, also, associated like the preceding, with
catastrophes and wars, and especially with the dreaded last
hours of the race. That of 1527 is described by Ambroise
Paré, and by Simon Goulart, as formed of severed heads,
poignards and bloody clouds. The comet of 1531 was
thought to herald the death of Louise of Savoy, mother of
Francis I., and this princess shared the popular superstition
in reference to evil stars: "Behold!" she exclaimed from
her bed, on perceiving the comet through the window,
"behold an omen which is not given to one of low degree.

God sends it as a warning to us. Let us prepare to meet death." Three days after, she died. But the famous comet of Charles v., appearing in 1556, was perhaps the most memorable of all. It had been identified as the comet of 1264, and its return was announced for 1848. But it did not reappear.

The comets of 1577, 1607, 1652 and 1665 were the subjects of endless commentaries, forming a library by themselves. At the last of these Alphonso vi., king of Portugal, angrily discharged his pistol, with the most grotesque defiance. Pierre Petit, by order of Louis xiv., published a work designed to counteract the foolish, and political, apprehensions excited by comets. This illustrious king desired to be without a rival, the only sun, "Nec pluribus impar!" and would not admit the supposition that the glory of France could be imperilled even by a celestial phenomenon.

One of the greatest comets which ever struck the imagination of men was assuredly the famous comet of 1680, to which Newton devoted so much attention. "It issued," said Lemonnier, "with a frightful velocity from the depths of space and seemed falling directly into the sun and was seen to vanish with an equal velocity. It was visible for four months. It approached quite near to the earth, and Whiston ascribed the deluge to its former appearance." Bayle wrote a treatise to prove the absurdity of beliefs founded on these portents. Madame de Sévigné writing to her cousin, Count de Bussy-Rabutin, says : " We have a comet of enormous size ; its tail is the most beautiful object conceivable. Every person of note is alarmed and believes that heaven, interested in their fate, sends them a warning in this comet. They say that the courtiers of Cardinal Mazarin, who is despaired of by his physicians believe this prodigy is in honor of his passing away, and tell him of the terror with which it has inspired them. He had the sense to laugh at them, and to reply facetiously that the comet did him too much honor. In truth we ought all to agree with him, for human pride assumes too much when it believes that death is attended by such signs from heaven."

We see that comets were gradually losing their prestige. Yet we read in a treatise of the astronomer Bernouilli this singular remark : " If the head of the comet be not a visible sign of the anger of God, *the tail may well be.*"

Fear of the end of the world was reawakened by the appearance of comets in 1773 ; a great panic spread throughout Europe, and Paris itself was alarmed. Here is an extract from the memoirs of Bachaumont, accessible to every reader :

" May 6th, 1773. In the last public meeting of the Academy of Sciences, M de Lalande was to read by far the most interesting paper of all ; this, however, he was not able to do, for lack of time. It concerned the comets which, by approaching the earth, may cause revolutions,

and dealt especially with that one whose return is expected
in eighteen years. But although he affirmed that it was
not one of those which would harm the earth, and that,
moreover, he had observed that one could not fix, with any
exactness, the order of such occurrences, there exists,
nevertheless, a very general anxiety.

"May 9th. The cabinet of M. de Lalande is filled with
the curious who come to question him concerning the
above memoir, and, in order to reassure those who have
been alarmed by the exaggerated rumors circulated about
it, he will doubtless be forced to make it public. The
excitement has been so great that some ignorant fanatics
have besought the archbishop to institute prayers for forty
hours, in order to avert the deluge which menaces us;
and this prelate would have authorized these prayers, had
not the Academy shown him the ridicule which such a
step would produce.

"May 14th. The memoir of M. de Lalande has appeared. He says that it is his opinion that, of the sixty
known comets, eight, by their near approach to the earth,
might produce a pressure such that the sea would leave its
bed and cover a part of the world."

In time, the excitement died away. The fear of comets
assumed a new form. They were no longer regarded as
indications of the anger of God, but their collision with
the earth was discussed from a scientific point of view, and
these collisions were not considered free of danger. At the

close of the last century, Laplace stated his views on this question, in the forcible language which we have quoted in Chapter II.

In this century, predictions concerning the end of the world have several times been associated with the appearance of comets. It was announced that the comet of Biela, for example, would intersect the earth's orbit on October 29, 1832, which it did, as predicted. There was great excitement. Once more the end of things was declared at hand. Humanity was threatened. What was going to happen?

The orbit, that is to say the path, of the earth had been confounded with the earth itself. The latter was not to reach that point of its orbit traversed by the comet until November 30th, more than a month after the comet's passage, and the latter was at no time to be within 20,000,000 leagues of us. Once more we got off with a fright.

It was the same in 1857. Some prophet of ill omen had declared that the famous comet of Charles v., whose periodic time was thought to be three centuries, would return on the 13th of June of that year. More than one timid soul was rendered anxious, and the confessionals of Paris were more than usually crowded with penitents. Another prediction was made public in 1872, in the name of an astronomer, who, however, was not responsible for it —M. Plantamour, director of the Geneva observatory.

As in the case of comets, so with other unusual phenomena, such as total solar eclipses, mysterious suns appearing
suddenly in the skies, showers of shooting stars, great
volcanic eruptions accompanied with the darkness of
night and seeming to threaten the burial of the world in
ashes, earthquakes overthrowing and engulfing houses and
cities—all these grand and terrible events have been connected with the fear of an immediate and universal end of
men and things.

The history of eclipses alone would suffice to fill a volume, no less interesting than the history of comets.   Con-
fining our attention to a modern example, one of the last
total eclipses of the sun, visible in France, that of August
12, 1654, had been foretold by astronomers, and its announcement had produced great alarm.   For some it
meant the overthrow of states and the fall of Rome; for
others it signified a new deluge; there were those who
believed that nothing less than the destruction of the world
by fire was inevitable; while the more collected anticipated
the poisoning of the atmosphere.   Belief in these dreaded
results were so widespread, that, in order to escape them,
and by the express order of physicians, many terrified people shut themselves up in closed cellars, warmed and perfumed.   We refer the reader, especially, to the second
evening of Les Mondes of Fontenelle.   Another writer of
the same century, Petit, to whom we referred a moment
ago, in his Dissertation on the Nature of Comets says, that

PEOPLE SEEKING REFUGE IN CLOSED CELLARS.

the consternation steadily increased up to the fatal day, and that a country curate, unable to confess all who believed their last hour was at hand, at sermon time told his parishioners not to be in such haste, for the eclipse had been put off for a fortnight; and these good people were as ready to believe in the postponement of the eclipse as they had been in its malign influence.

At the time of the last total solar eclipses visible in France, namely, those of May 12, 1706; May 22, 1724, and July 8, 1842, as also of the partial ones of October 9, 1847; July 28, 1851; March 15, 1858; July 18, 1860, and December 22, 1870, there was more or less apprehension on the part of the timid; at least, we know, from trustworthy sources, that in each of these cases these natural phenomena were interpreted by a certain class in Europe as possible signs of divine wrath, and in several religious educational establishments the pupils were requested to offer up prayers as the time of the eclipse drew near. This mystical interpretation of the order of nature is slowly disappearing among enlightened nations, and the next total eclipse of the sun, visible in southern France on May 28, 1900, will probably inspire no fear on the French side of the Pyrenees; but it might be premature to make the same statement regarding those who will observe it from the Spanish side of the mountains.

Among uncivilized people these phenomena excite today the same terror which they once did among us. This fact is frequently attested by travellers, especially in Africa. During the eclipse of July 18, 1860, in Algeria, men and women resorted to prayer or fled affrighted to their homes. During the eclipse of July 29, 1878, which was total in the United States, a negro, suddenly crazed with terror, and persuaded that the end of the world was coming, cut the throats of his wife and children.

It must be admitted that such phenomena are well calculated to overwhelm the imagination. The sun, the god of day, the star upon whose light we are dependent, grows dim ; and, just before it becomes extinguished, takes on a sickly and mournful hue. The light of the sky pales, the animal creation is stricken with terror, the beast of burden falters at his task, the dog flees to its master, the hen retreats with her brood to the coop, the birds cease their songs, and have been seen even to drop dead with fright. Arago relates that during the total eclipse of the sun at Perpignan, on July 8, 1842, twenty thousand spectators were assembled, forming an impressive spectacle. "When the solar disc was nearly obscured, an irresistible anxiety took possession of everybody ; each felt the need of sharing his impressions with his neighbor. A deep murmur arose, like that of the far away sea after a storm. This murmur deepened as the crescent of light grew less, and when it had disappeared and sudden darkness had supervened, the silence which ensued marked this phase of the eclipse as accurately as the

pendulum of our astronomical clock. The magnificence
of the spectacle triumphed over the petulance of youth,
over the frivolity which some people mistake for a sign
of superiority, over the indifference which the soldier
frequently assumes. A profound silence reigned also in
the sky : the birds had ceased their songs. After a solemn interval of about two minutes, joyous transports and
frantic applause greeted with the same spontaneity the
first reappearance of the solar rays, and the melancholy and
indefinable sense of depression gave way to a deep and un-
feigned exultation which no one sought to moderate or
repress."

Every one who witnessed this phenomenon, one of the
most sublime which nature offers, was profoundly moved,
and took away with him an impression never to be forgotten. The peasants especially were terrified by the darkness, as they believed that they were losing their sight. A
poor child, tending his flock, completely ignorant of what
was coming, saw the sun slowly growing dim in a cloudless sky. When its light had entirely disappeared the
poor child, completely carried away by terror, began to cry
and call for help. His tears flowed again when the first
ray of light reappeared. Reassured, he clasped his hands,
crying, "O, beautiful sun ! "

Is not the cry of this child the cry of humanity ?

So long as eclipses were not known to be the natural
consequences of the motion of the moon about the earth,

and before it was understood that their occurrence could be predicted with the utmost precision, it was natural that they should have produced a deep impression and been associated with the idea of the end of the world. The same is true of other celestial phenomena and notably of the sudden appearance of unknown suns, an event much rarer than an eclipse.

The most celebrated of these appearances was that of 1572. On the 11th of November of that year, about a month after the massacre of St. Bartholomew, a brilliant star of the first magnitude suddenly appeared in the con-

"O, BEAUTIFUL SUN !"

stellation of Cassiopeia. The stupefaction was general, not only on the part of the public, to which it was visible every night in the sky, but also on the part of scientists, who could not explain its appearance. Astrologers found a solution of the enigma in the assertion that it was the star of the Magi, whose reappearance announced the return of the Son of God, the last judgment and the resurrection. This statement made a deep impression upon all classes of society. The star gradually diminished in splendor, and at the end of about eighteen months went out, without having

caused any other disaster than that which human folly
itself adds to the misery of a none too prosperous planet.
Science records several apparitions of this nature, but the
above was the most remarkable. A like agitation has accompanied all the grand phenomena of nature, especially
those which have been unforeseen. In the chronicles of the
middle ages, and even in more recent memoirs, we read of
the terror which the aurora borealis, showers of shooting
stars and the fall of meteorites have produced among the
alarmed spectators. Recently, during the meteor shower
of November 27, 1872, when the sky was filled with more
than forty thousand meteorites belonging to the dispersed
comet of Biela, women of the lower classes, at Nice especially, as also at Rome, in their excitement sought information of those whom they thought able to explain the
cause of these celestial fireworks, which they had at once
associated with the end of the world and with the fall of
the stars, which it was foretold would usher in that last
great event.

Earthquakes and volcanic eruptions have sometimes attained such proportions as to lead to the fear that the end
of the world was at hand. Imagine the state of mind of
the inhabitants of Herculaneum and of Pompeii when the
eruption of Vesuvius buried them in showers of ashes!
Was not this for them the end of the world? And more
recently, were not those who witnessed the eruption of
Krakatoa of the same opinion? Impenetrable darkness

lasting eighteen hours, an atmosphere like a furnace, filling the eyes, nose and ears with ashes, the deep and incessant cannonade of the volcano, the falling of pumice stones from the black sky, the terrible scene illuminated only at intervals by the lurid lightning or the fire-balls on the spars and rigging of vessels, the thunder echoing from cloud and sea with an infernal musketry, the shower of ashes turning into a deluge of mud—this was the experience of the passengers of a Java vessel during the night of eighteen hours, from the 26th to the 28th of August, 1883, when a portion of the island of Krakatoa was hurled into the air, and the sea, after having first retreated, swept upon the shore to a height of thirty-five meters and to a distance of from one to ten kilometers over a coast-line of five hundred kilometers, and in the reflux carried away with it the four cities, Tjiringin, Mérak, Telok-Bétong and Anjer, and the entire population of the region, more than forty thousand souls. For a long time the progress of vessels was hindered by floating bodies inextricably interlaced; and human fingers, with their nails, and fragments of heads, with their hair were found in the stomachs of fishes. Those who escaped, or who saw the catastrophe from some vessel, and lived to welcome again the light of day, which had seemed forever extinguished, relate in terror with what resignation they expected the end of the world, persuaded that its very foundations were giving way and that the knell of a universal doom had sounded. One eye-witness assures us that he

would not again pass through such an experience for all
the wealth that could be imagined. The sun was extinguished and death seemed to reign sovereign over nature.
This eruption, moreover, was of such terrific violence that
it was heard through the earth at the antipodes; it reached
an altitude of twenty thousand meters, producing an atmospheric disturbance which made the circuit of the entire
globe in thirty-five hours (the barometer fell four milomet-
ers in Paris even), and left for more than a year in the
upper layers of the atmosphere a fine dust, which, illumined by the sun, gave rise to those magnificent twilight
displays admired so much throughout the world.

These are formidable disturbances, partial ends of the
world. Certain earthquakes deserve citation with these
terrible volcanic eruptions, so disastrous have been their
consequences. In the earthquake of Lisbon, November 1,
1755, thirty thousand persons perished; the shock was felt
over an area four times as large as that of Europe. When
Lima was destroyed, October 28, 1724, the sea rose twenty-
seven meters above its ordinary level, rushed upon the city
and erased it so completely that not a single house was left.
Vessels were found in the fields several kilometers from the
shore. On December 10, 1869, the inhabitants of the city
of Onlah, in Asia Minor, alarmed by subterranean noises
and a first violent trembling of the earth, took refuge on a
neighboring hilltop, whence, to their stupefaction, they saw
several crevasses open in the city which within a few

"FLOATING BODIES INEXTRICABLY INTERLACED."

moments entirely disappeared in the bowels of the earth. We have direct evidence that under circumstances far less dramatic, as for example on the occasion of the earthquake at Nice, February 23, 1887, the idea of the end of the world was the very first which presented itself to the mind.

The history of the earth furnishes a remarkable number of like dramas, catastrophes of a partial character, threatening the world's final destruction. It is fitting that we should devote a moment to the consideration of these great phenomena, as also to the history of that belief in the end of the world which has appeared in every age, though modified by the progress of human knowledge. Faith has in part disappeared; mystery and superstition, which struck the imagination of our ancestors, and which has been so curiously represented in the portals of our great cathedrals, and in the sculpture and painting inspired by Christian traditions, this theological aspect of the last great day, has given place to the scientific study of the probable life of the solar system to which we belong. The geocentric and anthropocentric conception of the universe, which makes man the center and end of creation, has become gradually transformed and has at last disappeared; for we know that our humble planet is but an island in the infinite, that human history has thus far been founded on pure illusions, and that the dignity of man consists in his intellectual and moral worth. Is not the destiny and sovereign end of the human mind the exact knowledge of things, the search after truth ?

During the nineteenth century, evil prophets, more or less sincere, have twenty-five times announced the end of the world, basing their prophecies upon cabalistic calculations destitute of serious foundation. Like predictions will recur so long as the race exists.

But this historic interlude, although opportune, has for a moment interrupted our narrative. Let us hasten to return to the twenty-fifth century, for we have reached its most critical moment.

CHAPTER VII.

INEXORABLY, with a fatality no power could arrest, like a projectile speeding from the mouth of a cannon toward the target, the comet continued to advance, following its appointed path, and hurrying, with an ever-increasing velocity, toward the point in space at which the earth would be found on the night of July 14–15. The final calculations were absolutely without error. These two heavenly bodies—the earth and the comet—were to meet like two trains, rushing headlong upon each other, with resistless momentum, as if impelled to mutual destruction by an insatiable rage. But in the present instance the velocity of shock would be 865 times that of two express trains having each a speed of one hundred kilometers per hour.

During the night of July 13–14, the comet spread over nearly the entire sky, and whirlwinds of fire could be seen by the naked eye, eddying about an axis oblique to the zenith. The appearance was that of an army of flaming meteors, in whose midst the flashing lightning produced the effect of a furious combat. The burning star had a revolution of its own, and seemed to be convulsed with pain, like a living thing. Immense jets of flame issued from various centers, some of a greenish hue, others red as blood, while the most brilliant were of a dazzling whiteness. It was evident that the sun was acting powerfully upon this whirlpool of gases, decomposing certain of them, forming detonating compounds, electrifying the nearer portions, and repelling the smoke from about the immense nucleus which was bearing down upon the world. The comet itself emitted a light far different from the sunlight reflected by the enveloping vapors ; and its flames, shooting forth in ever-increasing volume, gave it the appearance of a monster, precipitating itself upon the earth to devour it. Perhaps the most striking feature of this spectacle was the absence of all sound. At Paris, as elsewhere, during that eventful night, the crowd instinctively maintained silence, spellbound by an indescribable fascination, endeavoring to catch some echo of the celestial thunder— but not a sound was heard.

The moon rose full, showing green upon the fiery background of the sky, but without brilliancy and casting no shadows. The night was no more night, for the stars had disappeared, and the sky glowed with an intense light.

The comet was approaching the earth with a velocity of 41,000 meters per second, or 2460 kilometers per minute, that is, 147,600 kilometers per hour; and the earth was itself travelling through space, from west to east, at the rate of 29,000 meters per second, 1740 kilometers per minute, or 104,400 kilometers per hour, in a direction oblique to the orbit of the comet, which for any meridian appeared at midnight in the northeast. Thus, in virtue of their velocities, these two celestial bodies were nearing each other at the rate of 173,000 kilometers per hour. When observation, which was in entire accord with the computations previously made, established the fact that the nucleus of the comet was at a distance no greater than that of the moon, everyone knew that two hours later the first phenomena of the coming shock would begin.

Contrary to all expectation, Friday and Saturday, the 13th and 14th of July were, like the preceding days, wonderfully beautiful; the sun shone in a cloudless sky, the air was tranquil, the temperature rather high, but cooled by a light, refreshing breeze. Nature was in a joyous mood, the country was luxuriant with beauty, the streams murmured in the valleys, the birds sang in the woods; but the dwelling places of man were heartrendingly sad. Humanity was prostrated with terror, and the impassible calm of nature stood over against the agonizing fear of the human heart in painful and harrowing contrast.

Two millions of people had fled to Australia from Paris, London, Vienna, Berlin, St. Petersburg, Rome and Madrid. As the day of collision approached, the Trans-Atlantic Navigation company had been obliged to increase three-fold, fourfold, and even tenfold, the number of air-ships, which settled like flocks of birds upon San Francisco, Honolulu, Noumea, and the Australian cities of Mel-

PEOPLE LEAVING PARIS.

bourne, Sidney and Pax. But this exodus of millions represented only the fortunate minority, and their absence was scarcely noticed in the towns and villages, swarming with restless and anxious life.

Haunted by the fear of unknown perils, for several nights no one had been able to close their eyes, or even dared to go to bed. To do so, seemed to court the last sleep and to abandon all hope of awakening again. Every face was livid with terror, every eye was sunken ; the hair was dishevelled, the countenance haggard and stamped with the impress of the most frightful anguish which had ever preyed upon the human soul.

The atmosphere was growing drier and warmer. Since the evening before, no one had bethought himself of food, and the stomach, usually so imperious in its demands, craved for nothing. A burning thirst was the first physiological effect of the dryness of the atmosphere, and the most self-restrained sought, in every possible way, to quench it, though without success. Physical pain had begun its work, and was soon to dominate mental suffering. Hour by hour, respiration became more difficult, more exhausting and more painful. Little children, in the presence of this new suffering, appealed in tears to their mothers.

At Paris, London, Rome and St. Petersburg, in every capital, in every city, in every village, the terrified population wandered about distractedly, like ants when their

"STRANGERS TO THE UNIVERSAL PANIC."

habitations are disturbed. All the business of ordinary life was neglected, abandoned, forgotten; every project was set aside. No one cared any longer for anything, for his house, his family, his life. There existed a moral prostration and dejection, more complete than even that which is produced by sea-sickness. Some few, abandoning themselves to the exaltation of love, seemed to live only for each other, strangers to the universal panic.

Catholic and Protestant churches, Jewish synagogues, Greek chapels, Mohammedan mosques and Buddhist tem-

ples, the sanctuaries of the new Gallican religion—in
short, the places of assembly of every sect into which the id-
iosyncrasies of belief had divided mankind, were thronged
by the faithful on that memorable day of Friday, July
13th; and even at Paris the crowds besieging the portals
were such that no one could get near the churches, within
which were to be seen vast multitudes, all prostrate upon
the ground. Prayers were muttered in low tones, but no
chant, no organ, no bell was to be heard. The confessionals were surrounded by penitents, waiting their turn,
as in those early days of sincere and naïve faith described
by the historians of the middle ages.

Everywhere on the streets and on the boulevards the
same silence reigned; not a sound disturbed the hush,
nothing was sold, no paper was printed; aviators, aeroplanes, dirigible balloons were no more to be seen; the
only vehicles passing were the hearses bearing to the
crematories the first victims of the comet, already numerous. The days of July 13th and 14th had passed without
incident, but with what anxiety the fateful night was
awaited! Never, perhaps, had there been so magnificent
a sunset, never a sky so pure! The orb of day seemed
to go down in a sea of gold and purple; its red disc disappeared below the horizon, but the stars did not rise—
and night did not come! To the daylight succeeded a
day of cometary and lunar splendor, illuminated by a
dazzling light, recalling that of the aurora borealis, but

more intense, emanating from an immense blazing focus, which had not been visible during the day because it had been below the horizon, but which would certainly have rivalled the sun in brilliancy. Amid the universal plaint of nature, this luminous center rose in the west almost at the same time with the full moon, which climbed the sky with it like a sacrificial victim ascending the funeral pyre. The moon paled as it mounted higher, but the comet increased in brightness as the sun sank below the western horizon, and now, when the hour of night had come, it reigned supreme, a vaporous, scarlet sun, with flames of yellow and green, like immense extended wings. To the terrified spectator it seemed some enormous giant, taking sovereign possession of earth and sky.

Already the cometary fringes had invaded the lunar orbit. At any moment they would reach the rarer limits of the earth's atmosphere, only two hundred kilometers away.

Then everyone beheld, as it were, a vast conflagration, kindled over the whole extent of the horizon, throwing skyward little violet flames, and almost immediately the brilliancy of the comet diminished, doubtless because just before touching the earth it had entered into the shadow of the planet and had lost that part of its light which came from the sun. This apparent decrease in brilliancy was chiefly due to contrast, for when the eye, less dazzled, had become accustomed to this new light, it seemed almost as intense as the former, but of a sickly, lurid, sepulchral hue. Never before had the earth been bathed in such a light, which at first seemed to be colorless, emitting lightning flashes from its pale and wan depths. The dryness of the air, hot as the breath of a furnace, became intolerable, and a horrible odor of sulphur, probably due to the super-electrified ozone, poisoned the atmosphere. Everyone believed his last hour was at hand. A terrible cry dominated every other sound. The earth is on fire ! The earth is on fire ! Indeed, the entire horizon was now illuminated by a ring of bluish flame, surrounding the earth like the flames of a funeral pile. This, as had been predicted, was the carbonic-oxide, whose combustion in the air produced carbonic-anhydride.

Suddenly, as the terrified spectator gazed silent and awestruck, holding his very breath in a stupor of fear, the vault of heaven seemed rent asunder from zenith to horizon, and from this yawning chasm, as from an enormous mouth, was vomited forth jets of dazzling greenish flame, enveloping the earth in a glare so blinding, that all who had not already sought shelter, men and women, the old and the young, the bold as well as the timid, all rushed with the impetuosity of an avalanche to the cellarways, already choked with people. Many were crushed to death, or succumbed to apoplexy, aneurismal ruptures, and wild delirium resulting in brain fever.

On the terraces and in the observatories, however, the

astronomers had remained at their posts, and several had succeeded in taking an uninterrupted series of photographs of the sky changes ; and from this time, but for a very brief interval, with the exception of a few courageous spirits, who dared to gaze upon the awful spectacle from behind the windows of some upper apartment, they were the sole witnesses of the collision.

Computation had indicated that the earth would penetrate the heart of the comet as a bullet would penetrate a cloud, and that the transit, reckoning from the first instant of contact of the outer zones of the comet's atmosphere with those of the earth, would consume four and one-half hours,—a fact easily established, inasmuch as the comet, having a diameter about sixty-five times that of the earth, would be traversed, not centrally, but at one-quarter of the distance from the center, with a velocity of about 173,000 kilometers per hour. Nearly forty minutes after the first instant of contact, the heat of this incandescent furnace, and the horrible odor of sulphur, became so suffocating that a few moments more of such torture would have sufficed to destroy every vestige of life. Even the astronomers crept painfully from room to room within the observatories which they had endeavored to close hermetically, and sought shelter in the cellars ; and the young computor, whose acquaintance we have already made, was the last to remain on the terrace, at Paris,—a few seconds only, but long enough to witness the explosion of a for-

midable bolide, which was rushing southward with the
velocity of lightning. But strength was lacking for further observations. One could breathe no longer. Besides
the heat and the dryness, so destructive to every vital
function, there was the carbonic-oxide which was already
beginning to poison the atmosphere. The ears were filled
with a dull, roaring sound, the heart beat ever more and

"A FIERY RAIN FELL FROM EVERY QUARTER
OF THE SKY."

more violently; and still
this choking odor of
sulphur! At the same
time a fiery rain fell
from every quarter of
the sky, a rain of shoot-
ing stars, the immense
majority of which did
not reach the earth, al-
though many fell upon
the roofs, and the fires
which they kindled
could be seen in every
direction. To these fires
from heaven the fires of earth now made answer, and
the world was surrounded with electric flashes, as by an
army. Everyone, without thinking for an instant of
flight, had abandoned all hope, expecting every moment
to be buried in the ruins of the world, and those who
still clung to each other, and whose only consolation was

that of dying together, clung closer in a last embrace.

But the main body of the celestial army had passed, and a sort of rarefaction, of vacuum, was produced in the atmosphere, perhaps as the result of meteoric explosions ; for suddenly the windows were shattered, blown outwards, and the doors opened of themselves. A violent wind arose, adding fury to the conflagration. Then the rain fell in torrents, but reanimating at the same time the extinguished hope of life, and waking mankind from its nightmare.

" *The XXVth Century ! Death of the Pope and all the bishops ! Fall of the comet at Rome ! Paper, sir ?* "

Scarcely a half hour had passed before people began to issue from their cellars, feeling again the joy of living, and recovering gradually from their apathy. Even before one had really begun to take any account of the fires which were still raging, notwithstanding the deluge or rain, the scream of the newsboy was heard in the hardly awakened streets. Everywhere, at Paris, Marseilles, Brussels, London, Vienna, Turin and Madrid, the same news was being shouted, and before caring for the fires which were spreading on every side, everyone bought the popular one-cent sheet, with its sixteen illustrated pages fresh from the press.

" *The Pope and the cardinals crushed to death ! The sacred college destroyed by the comet ! Extra ! Extra !* "

The newsboys drove a busy trade, for everyone was

12

" EXTRA !"

anxious to know the truth of these an-
nouncements, and eagerly bought the
great popular socialistic paper.

This is what had taken place. The
American Hebrew, to whom we have already referred, and who, on the preceding Tuesday, had managed to make several millions by the reopening of the
Paris and Chicago exchanges, had not
for a moment yielded to despair, and, as
in other days, the monasteries had accepted bequests made
in view of the end of the world, so our indefatigable
speculator had thought best to remain at his telephone,
which he had caused to be taken down for the nonce into
a vast subterranean gallery, hermetically closed. Con-
trolling special wires uniting Paris with the principal cities
of the world, he was in constant communication with
them. The nucleus of the comet had contained within
its mass of incandescent gas a certain number of solid
uranolites, some of which measured several kilometers in
diameter. One of these masses had struck the earth not
far from Rome, and the Roman correspondent had sent
the following news by phonogram :

" All the cardinals and prelates of the council were
assembled in solemn fête under the dome of St. Peter. In
this grandest temple of Christendom, splendidly illuminated at the solemn hour of midnight, amid the pious invo-

cations of the chanting brotherhoods, the altars smoking with the perfumed incense, and the organs filling the recesses of the immense church with their tones of thunder, the Pope, seated upon his throne, saw prostrate at his feet his faithful people from every quarter of the world ; but as he rose to pronounce the final benediction a mass of iron, half as large as the city itself, falling from the sky with the rapidity of lightning, crushed the assembled multitudes, precipitating them into an abyss of unknown depth, a veritable pit of hell. All Italy was shaken, and the roar of the thunder was heard at Marseilles."

The bolide had been seen in every city throughout Italy, through the showers of meteorites and the burning atmosphere. It had illumined the earth like a new sun with a brilliant red light, and a terrible rending had followed its fall, as if the sky had really been split from top to bottom. (This was the bolide which the young calculator of the observatory of Paris had observed when, in spite of her zeal, the suffocating fumes had driven her from the terrace.)

Seated at his telephone, our speculator received his despatches and gave his orders, dictating sensational news to his journal, which was printed simultaneously in all the principal cities of the world. A quarter of an hour later these despatches appeared on the first page of the xxvth Century, in New York, St. Petersburg and Melbourne, as also in the capitals nearer Paris ; an hour after the first edition a second was announced.

"*Paris in flames! The cities of Europe destroyed! Rome in ashes! Here's your XXVth Century, second edition!*"

And in this new edition there was a very closely written article, from the pen of an accomplished correspondent, dealing with the consequences of the destruction of the sacred college.

"*Twenty-fifth Century, fourth edition! New volcano in Italy! Revolution in Naples! Paper, sir?*"

The second had been followed by the fourth edition without any regard to a third. It told how a bolide, weighing ten thousand tons, or perhaps more, had fallen with the velocity above stated upon the solfatara of Pozzuoli, penetrating and breaking in the light and hollow crust of the ancient crater. The flames below had burst forth in a new volcano, which, with Vesuvius, illuminated the Elysian fields.

"*Twenty-fifth Century, sixth edition! New island in the Mediterranean! Conquests of England!*"

A fragment of the head of the comet had fallen into the Mediterranean to the west of Rome, forming an irregular island, fifteen hundred meters in length by seven hundred in width, with an altitude of about two hundred meters. The sea had boiled about it, and huge tidal waves had swept the shores. But there happened to be an Englishman nearby, whose first thought was to land in a creek of the newly formed island, and scaling a rock, to plant the British flag upon its highest peak.

Millions of copies of the journal of the famous speculator were distributed broadcast over the world during this night of July 14th, with accounts of the disaster, dictated by telephone from the office of its director, who had taken measures to monopolize every item of news. Everywhere these editions were eagerly read, even before the necessary precautions were taken to extinguish the conflagrations still raging. From the outset, the rain had afforded unexpected succor, yet the material losses were immense, notwithstanding the prevailing use of iron in building construction.

" *Twenty-fifth Century, tenth edition ! Great miracle at Rome !* "

What miracle, it was easy enough to explain. In this latest edition, the xxvth Century announced that its correspondent at Rome had given circulation to a rumor which proved to be without foundation ; that the bolide had not destroyed Rome at all, but had fallen quite a distance outside the city. St. Peter and the Vatican had been miraculously preserved. But hundreds of millions of copies were sold in every country of the world. It was an excellent stroke of business.

The crisis had passed. Little by little, men recovered their self-possession, rejoicing in the mere fact of living.

Throughout the night, the sky overhead was illuminated by the lurid light of the comet, and by the meteorites which still fell in showers, kindled on every side new

THE COUNCIL ASSEMBLED UNDER THE DOME OF ST. PETER'S.

conflagrations. When day came, about half past three in
the morning, more than three hours had passed since the
head of the comet had collided with the earth ; the
nucleus had passed in a southwesterly direction, and the
earth was still entirely buried in the tail. The shock had
taken place at eighteen minutes after midnight ; that is to
say, fifty-eight minutes after midnight, Paris time, exactly
as predicted by the president of the Astronomical society
of France, whose statement our readers may remember.

Although, at the instant of collision, the greater part of
the hemisphere on the side of the comet had been effected
by the constricting dryness, the suffocating heat and the
poisonous sulphurous odors, as well as by deadening
stupor, due to the resistance encountered by the comet
in traversing the atmosphere, the supersaturation of the
ozone with electricity, and the mixture of nitrogen protoxide with the upper air, the other hemisphere had experienced no other disturbance than that which followed
inevitably from the destroyed atmospheric equilibrium.
Fortunately, the comet had only skimmed the earth, and
the shock had not been central. Doubtless, also, the
attraction of the earth had had much to do with the fall
of the bolides in Italy and the Mediterranean. At all
events, the orbit of the comet had been entirely altered by
this perturbation, while the earth and the moon continued
tranquilly on their way about the sun, as if nothing had
happened. The orbit of the comet had been changed by

the earth's attraction from a parabola to an ellipse, its aphelion being situated near the ecliptic. When later statistics of the comet's victims were obtained, it was found that the number of the dead was one-fortieth of the population of Europe. In Paris alone, which extended over a part of the departments formerly known as the Seine and Seine-et-Oise, and which contained nine million inhabitants, there was more than two hundred thousand deaths.

Prior to the fatal week, the mortality had increased threefold, and on the 10th fourfold. This rate of increase had been arrested by the confidence produced by the sessions of the Institute, and had even diminished sensibly during Wednesday. Unfortunately, as the threatening star drew near, the panic had resumed its sway. On the following Thursday the normal mortality rate had increased fivefold, and those of weak constitution had succumbed. On Friday, the 13th, the day before the disaster, owing to privations of every kind, the absence of food and sleep, the heat and feverish condition which it induced, the effect of the excitement upon the heart and brain, the mortality at Paris had reached the hitherto unheard of figure of ten thousand ! On the eventful night of the 14th, owing to the crowded condition of the cellars, the vitiation of the atmosphere by the carbonic-oxide gas, and suffocation due to the drying up of the lining membrane of the throat, pulmonary congestion, anæsthesia, and arrest of the circulation, the victims were more numerous than those of the battles of former times, the total for that day reaching the enormous sum of more than one hundred thousand. Some of those mortally effected lived until the following day, and a certain number survived longer, but in a hopeless condition. Not until a week had elapsed was the normal death-rate re-established. During this disastrous month 17,500 children were born at Paris, but nearly all died. Medical statistics, subtracting from the general total the normal mean, based upon a death-rate of twenty for every one thousand inhabitants, that is, 492 per day, or 15,252 for the month, which represents the number of those who would have died independently of the comet, ascribed to the latter the difference between these two numbers, namely, 222,633 ; of these, more than one-half, or more than one hundred thousand, died of fear, by syncope, aneurisms or cerebral congestions.

But this cataclysm did not bring about the end of the world. The losses were made good by an apparent increase in human vitality, such as had been observed formerly after destructive wars ; the earth continued to revolve in the light of the sun, and humanity to advance toward a still higher destiny.

The comet had, above all, been the pretext for the discussion of every possible phase of this great and important subject—the end of the world.

GIRLS REFUSING TO MARRY.

CHAPTER I.

THE events which we have just described, and the discussions to which they gave rise, took place in the twenty-fifth century of the Christian era. Humanity was not destroyed by the shock of the comet, although this was the most memorable event in its entire history, and one never forgotten, notwithstanding the many transformations which the race has since undergone. The earth had continued to rotate and the sun to shine ; little children had become old men, and their places had been filled by others in the eternal succession of generations. Centuries and ages had succeeded each other, and humanity, slowly advancing in knowledge and happiness, through a thousand transitory interruptions, had reached its apogee and accomplished its destiny.

But how vast these series of transformations—physical and mental !

The population of Europe, from the year 1900 to the year 3000, had increased from 375 to 700 millions ; that of Asia, from 875 to 1000 millions ; that of the Americas, from 120 to 1500 millions ; that of Africa, from 75 to 200 millions ; that of Australia, from 5 to 60 millions ; which, for the total population of the globe, gives an increase of 2010 millions. And this increase had continued, with some fluctuations.

Language had become transformed. The never-ceasing progress of science and industry had created a large number of new words, generally of Greek derivation. At the same time, the English language had spread over the entire world. From the twenty-fifth to the thirtieth centuries, the spoken language of Europe was based upon a mixture of English, of French, and of Greek derivatives. Every effort to create artificially a new universal language had failed.

Long before the twenty-fifth century, war had disappeared, and it became difficult to conceive how a race which pretended to knowledge and reason could have endured so long the yoke of clever rascals who lived at its expense. In vain had later sovereigns proclaimed, in high-sounding words, that war was a divine institution ; that it was the natural result of the struggle for existence ; that it constituted the noblest of professions ; that patriotism was the chief of virtues. In vain were battle-fields called fields of honor ; in vain were the statues of the victors erected in the most populous cities. It was, at last, observed that, with the exception of certain ants, no animal species had set an example of such boundless folly as the human race ; that the struggle for life did not consist in slaughtering one another, but in the conquest of nature ; that all the resources of humanity were absolutely wasted in the bottomless gulf of standing armies ; and that the mere obligation of military service, as formulated by law, was an encroachment upon human liberty, so serious that, under the guise of honor, slavery had been re-established.

Men perceived that the military system meant the maintenance of an army of parasites and idlers, yielding a passive obedience to the orders of diplomats, who were simply speculating upon human credulity. In early times, war had been carried on between villages, for the advantage and glory of chieftains, and this kind of petty warfare still prevailed in the nineteenth century, between the villages of central Africa, where even young men and women, persuaded of their slavery, were seen, at certain times, to present themselves voluntarily at the places where they were to be sacrificed. Reason having, at last, begun to prevail, men had then formed themselves into provinces, and a warfare between provinces arose—Athens contending with Sparta, Rome with Carthage, Paris with Dijon ; and history had celebrated the glorious wars of the Duke of Burgundy against the king of France, of the Normans against the Parisians, of the Belgians against the Flemish, of the Saxons against the Bavarians, of the Venetians

against the Florentines, etc., etc. Later, nations had been
formed, thus doing away with provincial flags and boun-
daries; but men continued to teach their children to hate
their neighbors, and citizens were accoutred for the sole
purpose of mutual extermination. Interminable wars
arose, wars ceaselessly renewed, between France, England,
Germany, Italy, Spain, Austria, Russia, Turkey, etc. The
development of weapons of destruction had kept pace with
the progress of chemistry, mechanics, aeronautics, and
most of the other sciences, and theorists were to be found,
especially among statesmen, who declared that war was
the necessary condition of progress, forgetting that it was
only the sorry heritage of barbarism, and that the majority
of those who have contributed to the progress of science
and industry, electricity, physics, mechanics, etc., have all
been the most pacific of men. Statistics had proved that
war regularly claimed forty million victims per century,
1100 per day, without truce or intermission, and had
made 1200 million corpses in three thousand years. It
was not surprising that nations had been exhausted and
ruined, since in the nineteenth century alone they had
expended, to this end, the sum of 700,000 million francs.
These divisions, appealing to patriotic sentiments skillfully kept alive by politicians who lived upon them, long
prevented Europe from imitating the example of America
in the suppression of its armies, which consumed all its
vital forces and wasted yearly more than ten thousand

million francs of the resources acquired at such sacrifice by the laborer, and from forming a United States of Europe. But though man could not make up his mind to do away with the tinsel of national vanity, woman came to his rescue.

Under the inspiration of a woman of spirit, a league was formed of the mothers of Europe, for the purpose of educating their children, especially their daughters, to a horror of the barbarities of war. The folly of men, the frivolity of the pretexts which arrayed nations against each other, the knavery of statesmen who moved heaven and earth to excite patriotism and blind the eyes of peoples ; the absolute uselessness of the wars of the past and of that European equilibrium which was always disturbed and never established ; the ruin of nations ; fields of battle strewn with the dead and the mangled, who, an hour before, lived joyously in the bountiful sun of nature ; widows and orphans—in short, all the misery of war was forced upon the mind, by conversation, recital and reading. In a single generation, this rational education had freed the young from this remnant of animalism, and inculcated a sentiment of profound horror for all which recalled the barbarism of other days. Still, governments refused to disarm, and the war budget was voted from year to year. It was then that the young girls resolved never to marry a man who had borne arms ; and they kept their vow.

The early years of this league were trying ones, even

for the young girls : for the choice of more than one fell
upon some fine-looking officer, and, but for the universal
reprobation, her heart might have yielded. There were, it
is true, some desertions ; but, as those who formed these
marriages were, from the outset, despised and ostracized
by society, they were not numerous. Public opinion was
formed, and it was impossible to stem the tide.

For about five years there was scarcely a single marriage
or union. Every citizen was a soldier, in France, in Germany, in Italy, in Spain, in every nation of Europe—all
ready for a confederation of States, but never recoiling
before questions represented by the national flag. The
women held their ground ; they felt that truth was on
their side, but their firmness would deliver humanity from
the slavery which oppressed it, and that they could not
fail of victory. To the passionate objurgations of certain
men, they replied : "No ; we will have nothing more to
do with fools ; " and, if this state of affairs continued, they
had decided to keep their vow, or to emigrate to America,
where, centuries before, the military system had disappeared.

The most eloquent appeals for disarmament were made
at every session to the committee of administrators of the
state, formerly called deputies or senators. Finally, after
a lapse of five years, face to face with this wall of feminine
opposition, which, day by day, grew stronger and more
impregnable, the deputies of every country, as if animated

by a common motive, eloquently advocated the cause of women, and that very week disarmament was voted in Germany, France, Italy, Austria and Spain.

It was spring-time. There was no disorder. Innumerable marriages followed. Russia and England had held aloof from the movement, the suffrage of women in these countries not having been unanimous. But as all the states of Europe were formed into a republic the ensuing year, uniting in a single confederated state, on the invitation of the government of the United States of Europe, these two great nations also decreed a gradual disarmament. Long before this time, India had been lost to England, and the latter had become a republic. As for Russia, the monarchical form of government still existed. It was then the middle of the twenty-fourth century, and from that epoch the narrow sentiment of patriotism was replaced by the general one of humanity.

Delivery from the ball and chain of military slavery, Europe had immediately gotten rid of the bureaucracy which had also exhausted nations, condemned to perish, as it were, by plethora. But for this a radical revolution was necessary. From that time on, Europe had advanced as by magic in a marvellous progress—social, scientific, artistic and industrial. Taxation, diminished by nine-tenths, served only for the maintenance of internal order, the security of life and property, the support of schools, and the encouragement of new researches. But individual initiative was far more effective than the old-time official centralization which for so many years had stifled individual effort, and bureaucracy was dead and buried.

At last one breathed freely, one lived. In order to pay 700,000 millions every century to citizens withdrawn from all productive work, and to maintain the bureaucracy, governments had been obliged to increase taxation to a fearful degree. The result was that everything was taxed ; the air one breathes, the water one drinks, the light and heat of the sun, bread, wine and every article of food, clothing, houses, the streets of cities, the country roads, animals, horses, oxen, dogs, cats, hens, rabbits, birds in cages, plants, flowers, musical instruments, pianos, organs, violins, zithers, flutes, trumpets, trades and professions, the married and the unmarried, children, furniture—everything, absolutely everything ; and this taxation had grown until it equalled the net product of all human labor, with the single exception of the "daily bread." Then, all work had ceased. It seemed thenceforth impossible to live. It was this state of affairs which led to the great social revolution of the international socialists, of which mention was made at the beginning of this book, and to others which followed it. But these upheavals had not definitely liberated Europe from the barbarism of by-gone days, and it was to the young women's league that humanity owes its deliverance.

The unification of nations, of ideas, of languages, had

"VOYAGES WERE MADE PREFERABLY BY AIR-SHIPS."

brought about also that of weights and measures. No
nation had resisted the universal adoption of the metric
system, based upon the dimensions of the planet itself. A
single kind of money was in circulation. One initial
meridian ruled in geography. This meridian passed
through the observatory of Greenwich, and at its antipode
the day changed its name at noon.

Nations which we call modern had vanished like those of
the past. France had disappeared in the twenty-eighth century, after an existence of about two thousand years. Germany disappeared in the thirty-second; Italy in the twenty-
ninth; England had spread over the surface of the ocean.

Meteorology had attained the precision of astronomy, and about the thirtieth century the weather could be predicted without error.

The forests, sacrificed to agriculture and the manufacture of paper, had entirely disappeared.

The legal rate of interest had fallen to one-half of one per cent.

Electricity had taken the place of steam. Railroads and pneumatic tubes were still in use, but only for the transportation of freight. Voyages were made preferably by dirigible balloons, aeroplanes and air-ships, especially in the daytime.

This very fact of aerial navigation would have done away with frontiers if the progress of reason had not already abolished them. Constant intercourse between all parts of the globe had brought about internationalism, and the absolutely free exchange of goods and ideas. Customhouses had been suppressed.

The telephonoscope disseminated immediately the most important and interesting news. A comedy played at Chicago or Paris could be heard and seen in every city of the world.

Astronomy had attained its end : the knowledge of the life of other worlds and the establishment of communication with them. All philosophy, all religion, was founded upon the progress of astronomy.

Marvellous instruments in optics and physics had been

invented. A new substance took the place of glass, and had yielded the most unexpected results to science. New natural forces had been conquered.

Social progress had been no less great than that of science. Machines driven by electricity had gradually taken the place of manual labor. At the same time the production of food had become entirely revolutionized. Chemical synthesis had succeeded in producing sugar, albumen, the amides and fats, from the air, water and vegetables, and, by skillfully varying the proportions, in forming the most advantageous combinations of carbon, hydrogen, oxygen and nitrogen, so that sumptuous repasts no longer consisted of the smoking remains of slaughtered animals—beef, veal, lamb, pork, chicken, fish and birds,—but were served amid the harmonies of music in rooms adorned with plants ever green and flowers ever in bloom, in an atmosphere laden with perfumes. Freed from the vulgar necessity of masticating meats, the mouth absorbed the principles necessary for the repair of organic tissues in exquisite drinks, fruits, cakes and pills.

About the thirtieth century, especially, the nervous system began to grow more delicate, and developed in unexpected ways. Woman was still somewhat more narrow-minded than man, and her mental operations differed from his as before (her exquisite sensibility responding to sentimental considerations before reason could act in the lower cells), and her head had remained smaller, her forehead narrower ; but the former was so elegantly placed upon a neck of such supple grace, and rose so nobly from the shoulders and the bust, that it compelled more than ever the admiration of man, not only as a whole, but also by the penetrating sweetness and beauty of the mouth and the light curls of its luxuriant hair. Although comparatively smaller than that of man, the head of woman had nevertheless increased in size with the exercise of the intellectual faculties ; but the cerebral circonvolutions had experienced the most change, having become more numerous and more pronounced in both sexes. In short, the head had grown, the body had diminished in size. Giants were no longer to be seen.

Four permanent causes had modified insensibly the human form ; the development of the intellectual faculties and of the brain, the decrease in manual labor and bodily exercise, the transformation of food, and the marriage system. The first had increased the size of the cranium as compared with the rest of the body ; the second had decreased the strength of the limbs; the third had diminished the size of the abdomen and made the teeth finer and smaller ; the tendency of the fourth had been rather to perpetuate the classic forms of human beauty : masculine beauty, the nobility of an uplifted countenance, and the graceful outlines of womanhood. About the two hundredth century of our era, a single race existed, rather small in stature, light colored, in which anthropologists might, perhaps, have discovered some form of Anglo-Saxon and Chinese descent.

Humanity had tended towards unity, one race, one language, one general government, one religion. There were no more state religions; only the voice of an enlightened conscience, and in this unity former anthropological differences had disappeared.

In former ages poets had prophesied that in the marvellous progress of things man would finally acquire wings, and fly through the air by his muscular force alone; but they had not studied the origin of anthropomorphic structure and had forgotten that for a man to have at the same time arms and wings, he must belong to a zoölogical order of sextupeds which does not exist on our planet; for man belongs to the quadrupeds, a type which has been gradually modified. But though he had not acquired new natural organs, he had acquired artificial ones, to say nothing of his physical transformation. He had conquered the region of the air and could soar in the sky by light apparatus, whose motor power was electricity, and the atmosphere had become his domain as it had been that of the birds. It is very probable that if in the course of ages a winged race could have acquired, by the development of its faculties of observation, a brain analogous to that of even the most primitive man, it would have soon dominated the human species and replaced it by a new one,—a winged race of the same zoölogical type as the

quadrupeds and bipeds. But the force of gravity is an
obstacle to any such organic development of the winged
species, and humanity, grown more perfect, had remained
master of the world.

At the same time, in the lapse of ages, the animal population of the globe had completely changed. The wild
species, lions, tigers, hyenas, panthers, elephants, giraffes,
kangaroos, as also whales and seals, had become extinct.

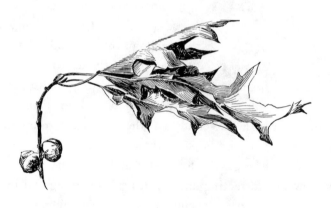

CHAPTER II.

ABOUT the one hundredth century of the Christian era all resemblance between the human race and monkeys had disappeared.

The nervous sensibility of man had become intensified to a marvellous degree. The sense of sight, of hearing, of smell, of touch, and of taste, had gradually acquired a delicacy far exceeding that of their earlier and grosser manifestations. Through the study of the electrical properties of living organisms, a seventh sense, the electric sense, was created outright, so to speak ; and everyone possessed the power of attracting and repelling both living and inert matter, to a degree depending upon the temperament of the individual. But by far the most important of all the senses, the one which played the greatest rôle in men's relation to each other, was the eighth, the psychic sense, by which communication at a distance became possible.

202

A glimpse has been had of two other senses also, but their development had been arrested from the very outset. The first had to do with the visibility of the ultra violet rays, so sensitive to chemical tests, but wholly invisible to the human eye. Experiments made in this direction has resulted in the acquisition of no new power, and had considerably impaired those previously enjoyed. The second was the sense of orientation ; but every effort made to develop it had proved a failure, notwithstanding the attempt to make use of the results of researches in terrestrial magnetism.

For some time past, the offspring of the once titled and aristocratic classes of society had formed a sickly and feeble race, and the governing body was recruited from among the more virile members of the lower class, who, however, were in their turn soon enervated by a worldly life. Subsequently, marriages were regulated on established principles of selection and heredity.

The development of man's intellectual faculties, and the cultivation of psychical science, had wrought great changes in humanity. Latent faculties of the soul had been discovered, faculties which had remained dormant for perhaps a million years, during the earlier reign of the grosser instincts, and, in proportion as food based upon chemical principles was substituted for the coarse nourishment which had prevailed for so long a time, these faculties came to light and underwent a brilliant development. As a mental operation, thought became a different thing from what it now is. Mind acted readily upon mind at a distance, by virtue of a transcendental magnetism, of which even children knew how to avail themselves.

The first interastral communication was with the
planet Mars, and the sec-
ond with Venus, the latter
being maintained to the
end of the world; the

"EVEN CHILDREN KNEW HOW TO AVAIL THEMSELVES OF IT."

former was interrupted by the death of the inhabitants
of Mars; whereas intercourse with Jupiter was only just
beginning as the human race neared its own end. A
rigid application of the principles of selection in the
formation of marriages had resulted in a really new race,
resembling ours in organic form, but possessing wholly
different intellectual powers. For the once barbarous and
often blind methods of medicine, and even of surgery, had
been substituted by those derived from a knowledge of
hypnotic, magnetic and psychic forces, and telepathy had
become a great and fruitful science.

Simultaneously with man the planet also had been transformed. Industry had produced mighty but ephemeral
results. In the twenty-fifth century, whose events we
have just described, Paris had been for a long time a sea-
port, and electric ships from the Atlantic, and from the
Pacific by the Isthmus of Panama, arrived at the quays of
the abbey of Saint Denis, beyond which the great capital
extended far to the north. The passage from the abbey
of Saint Denis to the port of London was made in a few
hours, and many travellers availed themselves of this
route, in preference to the regular air route, the tunnel,
and the viaduct over the channel. Outside of Paris the
same activity reigned; for, in the twenty-fifth century
also, the canal uniting the Mediterranean with the Atlantic had been completed, and the long detour by way of
the Straits of Gibraltar had been abandoned; and on the

other hand a metallic tube, for carriages driven by compressed air, united the Iberian republic, formerly Spain and Portugal, with western Algeria, formerly Morocco. Paris and Chicago then had nine million inhabitants, London, ten ; New York, twelve. Paris, continuing its growth toward the west from century to century, now extended from the confluence of the Marne beyond St. Germain. All great cities had grown at the expense of the country. Agricultural products were manufactured by electricity ; hydrogen was extracted from sea-water ; the energy of waterfalls and tides were utilized for lighting purposes at a distance ; the solar rays, stored in summer, were distributed in winter, and the seasons had almost disappeared, especially since the introduction of heat wells, which brought to the surface of the soil the seemingly inexhaustible heat of the earth's interior.

But what is the twenty-fifth century in comparison with the thirtieth, the fortieth, the hundredth !

Everyone knows the legend of the Arab of Kazwani, as related by a traveller of the thirteenth century, who at that time, moreover, had no idea of the duration of the epochs of nature. " Passing one day," he said, " by a very ancient and very populous city, I asked one of its inhabitants how long a time it had been founded. ' Truly,' he replied, ' it is a powerful city, but we do not know how long it has existed, and our ancestors are as ignorant upon this subject as we.'

THE CHINESE CAPITOL.

" Five centuries later I passed by the same spot, and could perceive no trace of the city. I asked a peasant who was gathering herbs on its former site, how long it had been destroyed. 'Of a truth,' he replied, 'that is a strange question. This field has always been what it now is.' 'But was there not formerly a splendid city here?' I asked. 'Never,' he answered, 'at least so far as we can judge from what we have seen, and our fathers have never told us of any such thing.'

" On my return five hundred years later to the same place I found it occupied by the sea ; on the shore stood a group of fishermen, of whom I asked at what period the land had been covered by the ocean. ' Is that question worthy of a man like you?' they replied ; 'this spot has always been such as you see it today.'

" At the end of five hundred years I returned again, and the sea had disappeared. I inquired of a solitary man whom I encountered, when this change had taken place; and he gave me the same reply.

" Finally, after an equal lapse of time, I returned once more, to find a flourishing city, more populous and richer in monuments than that which I had at first visited; and when I sought information as to its origin, its inhabitants replied : ' The date of its foundation is lost in antiquity. We do not know how long it has existed, and our fathers knew no more of this than we do.' "

How this fable illustrates the brevity of human memory and the narrowness of our horizons in time as well as in space ! We think that the earth has always been what it now is; we conceive with difficulty of the secular changes through which it has passed; the vastness of these periods overwhelms us, as in astronomy we are overwhelmed by the vast distances of space.

The time had come when Paris had ceased to be the capital of the world.

After the fusion of the United States of Europe into a single confederation, the Russian republic from St. Petersburg to Constantinople had formed a sort of barrier against the invasion of the Chinese, who had already established populous cities on the shores of the Caspian sea. The nations of the past having disappeared before the march of progress, and the nationalities of France, England, Germany, Italy and Spain having for the same reason passed away, communication between the east and west, between Europe and America, had become more and more easy ; and the sea being no longer an obstacle to the march of humanity, free now as the sun, the new territory of the vast continent of America had been preferred by industrial enterprise to the exhausted lands of western Europe, and already in the twenty-fifth century the center of civilization was located on the shores of Lake Michigan in a new Athens of nine million inhabitants, rivalling Paris. Thereafter the elegant French capital had followed the example of its predecessors, Rome, Athens, Memphis, Thebes, Nineveh and Babylon. The wealth, the resources of every kind, the great attractions, were elsewhere.

In Spain, Italy and France, gradually abandoned by their inhabitants, solitude spread slowly over the ruins of former cities. Lisbon had disappeared, destroyed by the sea ; Madrid, Rome, Naples and Florence were in ruins. A little later, Paris, Lyons and Marseilles were overtaken by the same fate.

Human types and languages had undergone such transformations that it would have been impossible for an ethnologist or a linguist to discover anything belonging to the past. For a long time neither Spanish, Portuguese, Italian, French, English nor German had been spoken. Europe had migrated beyond the Atlantic, and Asia had invaded Europe. The Chinese to the num-

14

ber of a thousand million had spread over western Europe. Mingling with the Anglo-Saxon race, they formed in some measure a new one. Their principal capital stretched like an endless street along each side of the canal from Bordeaux to Toulouse and Narbonne.

The causes which led to the foundation of Lutetia on an island in the Seine, which had raised this city of the Parisians to the zenith of its power in the twenty-fourth century, were no longer operative, and Paris had disappeared simultaneously with the causes to which it owed its origin and splendor. Commerce had taken possession of the Mediterranean and the great oceanic highways, and the Iberian canal had become the emporium of the world.

The littoral of the south and west of ancient France had been protected by dikes against the invasion of the sea, but, owing to the increase of population in the south and southwest, the north and northwest had been neglected, and the slow and continual subsidence of this region, observed ever since the time of Cæsar, had reduced its level below that of the sea ; and as the channel was ever widening, and the cliffs between Cape Helder and Havre were being worn away by the action of the sea, the Dutch dikes had been abandoned to the ocean, which had invaded the Netherlands, Belgium, and northern France, Amsterdam, Utrecht, Rotterdam, Antwerp, Versailles, Lille, Amiens and Rouen had sunk below the

THE RUINS OF PARIS.

water, and ships floated above their sea-covered ruins.

Paris itself, finally abandoned in the sixtieth century, when the sea had surrounded it as it now does Havre, was, in the eighty-fifth century, covered with water to the height of the towers of Notre Dame, and all that memorable plain, where were wrought out, during so many years, the most brilliant of the world's civilizations, was swept by angry waves.*

As in the case of languages, ideas, customs and laws, so, also, the manner of reckoning time had changed. It was still reckoned by years and centuries, but the Christian era had been discarded, as also the holy days of the calendar and the eras of the Mussulman, Jewish, Chinese and African chronologies. There was now a single calendar for the entire race, composed of twelve months, divided into four equal trimesters of three months of thirty-one, thirty, and thirty days, each trimester containing exactly thirteen weeks. New Year's Day was a fête day, and was not reckoned in with the year; every bisextile year there

---

* In the nineteenth century, researches in natural history had revealed the fact that secular vertical oscillations, vary with the locality, were taking place in the earth's crust, and had proved that, from prehistoric times, the soil of western and southern France had been slowly sinking and the sea slowly gaining upon the land. One after another, the islands of Jersey, of Minquiers, of Chaussey, of Écrehou, of Cezembre, of Mont-Saint-Michel, had been detached from the continent by the sea ; the cities of Is, Helion, Tommen, Portzmeûr, Harbour, Saint Louis, Monny, Bourgneuf, La Feillette, Paluel and Nazado had been buried beneath its waves, and the Armorican peninsula had slowly retreated before the advancing waters. The hour of this invasion by the sea had struck, from century to century. also for Herbavilla ; to the west of Nantes ; for Saint-Denis-Chef-de-Caux, to the north of Havre ; for Saint-Étienne-de-Paluel and for Gardoine, to the north of Dol ; for Tolente, to the west of Brest ; more than eighty habitable cities of Holland had been submerged in the eleventh century, etc., etc.   In other regions the reverse had taken place, and the sea had retired ; but to the north and west of Paris this double action of the subsidence of the land and the wearing away of the shores had, in less than seven thousand years, made Paris accessible to ships of the greatest tonnage.

were two. The week had been retained. Every year
commenced on the same day—Monday ; and the same
dates always corresponded to the same days of the week.
The year began with the vernal equinox all over the
world. The era, a purely astronomical division of time,
began with the coincidence of the December solstice with
perihelion, and was renewed every 25,765 years. This
rational method had succeeded the fantastic divisions of
time formerly in use.

The geographical features of France, of Europe and of
the entire world had become modified, from century to
century. Seas had replaced continents, and new deposits
at the bottom of the ocean covered the vanished ages,
forming new geological strata. Elsewhere, continents had
taken the place of seas. At the mouth of the Rhone,
for example, where the dry land had already encroached
upon the sea from Arles to the littoral, the continent
gained to the south ; in Italy, the deposits of the Po had
continued to gain upon the Adriatic, as those of the Nile,
the Tiber, and other rivers of later origin, had gained upon
the Mediterranean ; and in other places the dunes had increased, by various amounts, the domain of the dry land.
The contours of seas and continents had so changed that
it would have been absolutely impossible to make out the
ancient geographical maps of history.

The historian of nature does not deal with periods of
five centuries, like the Arab of the thirteenth century men-

tioned in the legend related a moment ago. Ten times this period would scarcely suffice to modify, sensibly, the configuration of the land, for five thousand years are but a ripple on the ocean of time. It is by tens of thousands of years that one must reckon if one would see continents sink below the level of seas, and new territories emerging into the sunlight, as the result of the secular changes in the level of the earth's crust, whose thickness and density varies from place to place, and whose weight, resting upon the still plastic and mobile interior, causes vast areas to oscillate. A slight disturbance of the equilibrium, an insignificant dip of the scales, a change of less than a hundred meters, often, in the length of the earth's diameter of twelve thousand kilometers, is sufficient to transform the surface of the world.

And if we examine the ensemble of the history of the earth, by periods of one hundred thousand years, for example, we see, that in ten of these great epochs, that is, in a million years, the surface of the globe has been many times transformed.

If we advance into the future a period of one or two million years, we witness a vast flux and reflux of life and things. How many times in this period of ten or twenty thousand centuries, how many times have the waves of the sea covered the former dwelling-places of man! How many times the earth has emerged anew, fresh and regenerated, from the abysses of the ocean! In primitive times,

when the still warm and liquid planet was covered only
by a thin shell, cooling on the surface of the burning
ocean within, these changes took place brusquely, by sudden breaking down of natural barriers, earthquakes, volcanic eruptions, and the uprising of mountain ranges.
Later, as this superficial crust grew thicker and became
consolidated, these transformations were more gradual;
the slow contraction of the earth had led to the formation
of hollow spaces within the solid envelope, to the falling
in of portions of this envelope upon the liquid nucleus,
and finally to oscillating movements which had changed
the profile of the continents. Later still, insensible modifications had been produced by external agents; on the
one hand the rivers, constantly carrying to their mouths
the débris of the mountains, had filled up the depths of
the sea and slowly increased the area of the dry land, making in time inland cities of ancient seaports; and on the
other hand, the action of the waves and of storms, constantly eating away the shores, had increased the area of
the ocean at the expense of the dry land. Ceaselessly the
geographical configuration of the shore had changed. For
the historian our planet had become another world. Everything had changed: continents, seas, shores, races, languages, customs, body and mind, sentiments, ideas—everything. France beneath the waves, the bottom of the Atlantic in the light of the sun, a portion of the United
States gone, a continent in the place of Oceanica, China

submerged ; death where was life, and life where was
death ; and everywhere sunk into eternal oblivion all
which had once constituted the glory and greatness of
nations.   If today one of us should emigrate to Mars, he
would find himself more at home than if, after the lapse
of these future ages, he should return to the earth.

CHAPTER III.

WHILE these great changes in the planets were taking place, humanity had continued to advance; for progress is the supreme law. Terrestrial life, which began with the rudimentary protozoans, without mouths, blind, deaf, mute and almost wholly destitute of sensation, had acquired successively the marvellous organs of sense, and had finally reached its climax in man, who, having also grown more perfect with the lapse of centuries, had risen from his primitive savage condition as the slave of nature to the position of a sovereign who ruled the world by mind, and who had made it a paradise of happiness, of pure contemplation, of knowledge and of pleasure.

Men had attained that degree of intelligence which enabled them to live wisely and tranquilly. After a general disarmament had been brought about, so rapid an increase in public riches and so great an amelioration in the well-being of every citizen was observed, that the efforts of intelligence and labor, no longer wasted by this intellectual suicide, had been directed to the conquest of new forces of nature and the constant improvement of civili-

zation. The human body had become insensibly transformed, or more exactly, transfigured.

Nearly all men were intelligent. They remembered
with a smile the childish ambitions of their ancestors
whose aspiration was to be some*one* rather than some*thing*,
and who had struggled so feverishly for outward show.
They had learned that happiness resides in the soul, that
contentment is found only in study, that love is the sun of
the heart, that life is short and ought not to be lived superficially ; and thus all were happy in the possession of
liberty of conscience, and careless of those things which
one cannot carry away.

Woman had acquired a perfect beauty. Her form had
lost the fullness of the Greek model and had become more
slender ; her skin was of a translucent whiteness ; her eyes
were illuminated by the light of dreams ; her long and
silky hair, in whose deep chestnut were blended all the
ruddy tints of the setting sun, fell in waves of rippling
light ; the heavy animal jaw had become idealized, the
mouth had grown smaller, and in the presence of its sweet
smile, at the sight of its dazzling pearls between the soft
rose of the lips, one could not understand how lovers could
have pressed such fervent kisses upon the lips of women
of earlier times, specimens of whose teeth, resembling
those of animals, had been preserved in the museums of
ethnography. It really seemed as if a new race had come
into existence, infinitely superior to that to which Aris-

totle, Kepler, Victor Hugo, Phryne, or Diana of Poictiers
had belonged.

Thanks to the progress in physiology, hygiene, and anti-
septic science, as well as to the general well-being and
intelligence of the race the duration of human life had
been greatly prolonged, and it was not unusual to see persons who had attained the age of 150 years. Death had
not been conquered, but the secret of living without growing old had been found, and the characteristics of youth
were retained beyond the age of one hundred.

But one fatherland existed on the planet, which, like a
chorus heard above the chords of some vast harmony,
marched onward to its high destiny, shining in the splendor of intellectual supremacy.

The internal heat of the globe, the light and warmth of
the sun, terrestrial magnetism, atmospheric electricity,
inter-planetary attraction, the psychic forces of the human
soul, the unknown forces which preside over destinies,—
all these science had conquered and controlled for the
benefit of mankind. The only limits to its conquests were
the limitations of the human faculties themselves, which,
indeed, are feeble, especially when we compare them with
those of certain extra-terrestrial beings.

All the results of this vast progress, so slowly and gradually acquired by the toil of centuries, must, in obedience
to a law, mysterious and inconceivable for the petty race
of man, reach at last their apogee, when further advance

becomes impossible. The geometric curve which represents this progress of the race, falls as it rises : starting
from zero, from the primitive nebulous cosmos, ascending
through the ages of planetary and human history to its
lofty summit, to descend thereafter into a night that
knows no morrow.

Yes ! all this progress, all this knowledge, all this happiness and glory, must one day be swallowed up in oblivion, and the voice of history itself be forever silenced.
Life had a be-ginning : it must have an end. The sun
of human hopes had ris-en, had ascend-ed victoriously
to its meridi-an, it was now to set and to disappear in
endless night. To what end then all this glory, all this
struggling, all these con-quests, all these vanities,
if light and life must come to an end ? Martyrs and
apostles, in every cause, have poured out blood upon the earth, destined also in its turn to perish.

Everything is doomed to decay, and death must re-

THE VILLAGE CEMETERY.

main the final sovereign of the world. Have you ever thought, in viewing a village cemetery, how small it is, to contain the generations buried there from time immemorable? Man existed before the last glacial epoch, which dates back 200,000 years; and the age of man extends over a period of more than 250,000 years. Written history dates from yesterday. Cut and polished flints have been found at Paris, proving the presence of man on the banks of the Seine long before the first historic record of the Gauls. The Parisians of the close of the nineteenth century walk upon ground consecrated by more than ten thousand years of ancestry. What remains of all who have swarmed in this forum of the world? What is left of the Romans, the Greeks, and the Asiatics, whose empires lasted for centuries? What remains of the millions who have existed? Not even a handful of ashes.

A human being dies every second, or about 86,000 a day, and an equal number, or to speak more exactly, a little more than 86,000 are born daily. This figure, true for the nineteenth century, applies to a long period, if we increase it proportionately to the time. The population of the globe has increased from epoch to epoch. In the time of Alexander there were perhaps a thousand million living beings on the surface of the earth. At the end of the nineteenth century fifteen hundred million; in the twenty-second century two thousand million; in the twenty-ninth three thousand million; at its maximum the population of the globe had reached one hundred thousand million. Then it had begun to decrease.

Of the innumerable human bodies which have lived, not one remains. All have been resolved into their elements, which have again formed new individuals.

All that fills the passing day—labor, pleasure, grief and happiness—vanishes with it into oblivion. Time flies, and the past exists no longer; what has been, has disappeared in the gulf of eternity. The visible world is vanishing every instant. Only the invisible is real and enduring.

During the ten million years of history, the human race, surviving generation after generation, as if it were a real thing, had been greatly modified from both a physical and moral point of view. It had always remained master of the world, and no new race had aspired to its sovereignty; for races do not come down from heaven or rise from hell; no Minerva is born full-armed, no Venus awakes full-grown in a shell of pearl on the seashore; everything grows, and the human race, with its long line of ancestry, was from the very beginning the natural result of the vital evolution of the planet. Under the law of progress, it had emerged from the limbo of animalism, and by the continued action of this same law of progress it had become gradually perfected, modified and refined.

But the time had come when the conditions of terrestrial life began to fail; when humanity, instead of advancing, was itself to enter upon its downward path.

The internal heat of the globe, still considerable in the nineteenth century, although it had ceased to have any effect upon surface temperature, which was maintained solely by the sun, had slowly diminished, and the earth had, at last, become entirely cold. This had not directly influenced the physical conditions of terrestrial life, which continued to depend upon the atmosphere and solar heat. The cooling of the earth cannot bring about the end of the world.

Imperceptibly, from century to century, the earth's surface had become levelled. The action of the rain, snow, frost and solar heat upon the mountains, the waters of torrents, rivulets and rivers, had slowly carried to the sea the débris of every continental elevation. The bottom of the sea had risen, and in nine million years the mountains had almost entirely disappeared. Meanwhile, the planet had grown old faster than the sun ; the conditions favorable to life had disappeared more rapidly than the solar light and heat.

This conception of the planet's future conforms to our present knowledge of the universe. Doubtless, our logic is radically incomplete, puerile even, in comparison with the real and eternal Truth, and might be justly compared with that of two ants talking together about the history of France. But, confessing the modesty which befits the finite in presence of the infinite, and acknowledging our nothingness as compared with the universe, we cannot avoid the necessity of appearing logical to ourselves ; we cannot assume that the abdication of reason is a better proof of wisdom than the use of it. We believe that an intelligent order presides over the universe and controls the destiny of worlds and their inhabitants ; that the larger members of the solar system must last longer than the lesser ones, and, consequently, that the life of each planet is not equally dependent upon the sun, and cannot, therefore, continue indefinitely, any more than the sun itself. Moreover, direct observation confirms this general conception of the universe. The earth, an extinct sun, has cooled more rapidly than the sun. Jupiter, so immense, is still in its youth. The moon, smaller than Mars, has reached the more advanced stages of astral life, perhaps even has reached its end. Mars, smaller than the earth, is more advanced than the earth and less so than the moon. Our planet, in its turn, must die before Jupiter, and this, also, must take place before the sun becomes extinct.

Consider, in fact, the relative sizes of the earth and the other planets. The diameter of Jupiter is eleven times that of the earth, and the diameter of the sun about ten times that of Jupiter. The diameter of Saturn is nine times that of the earth. It seems to us, therefore, natural to believe that Jupiter and Saturn will endure longer than our planet, Venus, Mars or Mercury, those pigmies of the system !

Events justified these deductions of science. Dangers lay in wait for us in the immensity of space; a thousand accidents might have befallen us, in the form of comets, extinct or flaming suns, nebulæ, etc. But the planet did not perish by an accident. Old age awaited the earth, as it waits for all other things, and it grew old faster than the sun. It lost the conditions necessary for life more rapidly than the central luminary lost its heat and its light.

During the long periods of its vital splendor, when, leading the chorus of the worlds, it bore on its surface an intelligent race, victors over the blind forces of nature, a protecting atmosphere, beneath which went on all the play of life and happiness, guarded its flourishing empires. An essential element of nature, water, regulated terrestrial life; from the very beginning this element had entered into the composition of every substance, vegetable, animal and human. It formed the active principle of atmospheric circulation; it was the chief agent in the changes of climate and seasons; it was the sovereign of the terrestrial state.

From century to century the quantity of water in the sea, the rivers and the atmosphere diminished. A portion of the rain water was absorbed by the earth, and did not return to the sea; for, instead of flowing into the sea over impermeable strata, and so forming either springs or subterranean and submarine watercourses, it had filtered deeper within the surface, insensibly filling every void, every fissure, and saturating the rocks to a great depth. So long as the internal heat of the globe was sufficient to prevent the indefinite descent of this water, and to convert it into vapor, a considerable quantity remained upon the surface ; but the time came when the internal heat of the globe was entirely dispersed in space and offered no obstacle to infiltration. Then the surface water gradually diminished ; it united with the rocks, in the form of hydrates, and thus disappeared from circulation.

Indeed, were the loss of the surface water of the globe to amount only to a few tenths of a millimeter yearly, in ten million years none would remain.

This vapor of water in the atmosphere had made warmth and life possible ; with its disappearance came cold and death. If at present the aqueous vapor of the atmosphere should disappear, the heat of the sun would be incapable of maintaining animal and vegetable life ; life which, moreover, could not exist, inasmuch as vegetables and animals are chiefly composed of water.*

The invisible vapor of water, distributed through the atmosphere, exercises the greatest possible influence on

---

* Of all terrestrial substances water has the greatest specific heat. It cools more slowly than any other. Its specific heat is four times greater than that of air. When the temperature of a kilogram of water falls one degree, it raises the temperature of four kilograms of air one degree. But water is seven hundred and seventy times heavier than air, so that if we compare two equal volumes of water and air, we find that a cubic meter of water, in losing one degree of temperature, raises the temperature of seven hundred and seventy times four, or 3080 cubic meters of air by the same amount. This is the explanation of the influence of the sea in modifying the climate of continents. The heat of summer is stored in the ocean and is slowly given out in winter. This explains why islands and seashores have no extremes of climate. The heat of summer is tempered by the breezes, and the cold of winter is alleviated by the heat stored in the water.

temperature. In quantity this vapor seems almost negligible, since oxygen and nitrogen alone form ninety-nine and one-half per cent. of the air we breathe; and the remaining one-half of one per cent. contains, besides the vapor of water, carbonic acid, ammonia and other substances. There is scarcely more than a quarter of one per cent. of aqueous vapor. If we consider the constituent atoms of the atmosphere, the physicist tells us that for two hundred atoms of oxygen and nitrogen there is scarcely one of water-vapor ; but this one atom has eighty times more absorptive energy than the two hundred others.

The radiant heat of the sun, after traversing the atmosphere, warms the surface of the earth. The heat waves reflected from the warmed earth are not lost in space. The aqueous vapor atoms, acting like a barrier, turn them back and preserve them for our benefit.

This is one of the most brilliant and the most fruitful discoveries of modern physics. The oxygen and nitrogen molecules of dry air do not oppose the radiation of heat ; but, as we have just said, one molecule of water-vapor possesses eighty times the absorptive energy of the other two hundred molecules of dry air, and consequently such a molecule is sixteen thousand times more efficacious in so far as the conservation of heat is concerned. So that it is the vapor of water and not the air, properly speaking, which regulates the conditions of life upon the earth.

If one should remove this vapor from the surrounding atmosphere, a loss of heat would go on at the surface similar to that which takes place in high altitudes, for the atmosphere would then be as powerless to retain heat as a vacuum is. A cold like that at the surface of the moon would be the result. The soil would still receive heat directly from the sun, but even during the daytime this heat would not be retained, and after sunset the earth would be exposed to the glacial cold of space, which appears to be about 273° below zero. Thus vegetable, animal and human life would be impossible, if it had not already become so, through the very disappearance of the water.

Certainly we may and must admit that water has not been so essential a condition of life on all the worlds of space as it has been upon our own. The resources of nature are not limited by human observation. There must be, there are, in the limitless realms of space, millions and millions of suns differing from ours, systems of worlds in which other substances, other chemical combinations, other physical and mechanical conditions, other environments, have produced beings absolutely unlike ourselves, living another life, possessed of other senses, differing in organization from ourselves far more than the fish or mollusk of the deep sea differs from the bird or the butterfly. But we are here studying the conditions of terrestrial life, and these conditions are

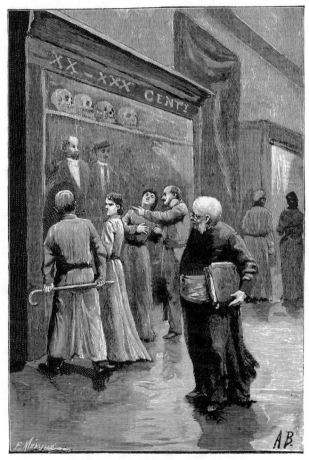

FOSSIL SPECIMENS OF THE XXTH. CENTURY.

determined by the constitution of the planet itself.

The gradual filtration of water into the interior of the earth, keeping pace with the radiation of the earth's original heat into space, the slow formation of oxides and hydrates, in about eight million years reduced by three-fourths the quantity of water in circulation on the earth's surface. As a consequence of the disappearance of continental elevations, whose débris, obeying passively the laws of gravity, were slowly carried by the rain, the wind, and the streams to the sea, the earth had become almost level and the seas more shallow ; but as evaporation and the formation of aqueous vapor goes on only from the surface and does not depend upon the depth, the atmosphere was still rich in vapor. The conditions of life upon the planet were then similar to those we now observe on Mars; where we see that great oceans have disappeared or have become mere inland seas of slight depth, that the continents are vast plains, that evaporation is active, that a considerable quantity of aqueous vapor still exists, that rains are rare, that snows abound in the polar regions and are almost entirely melted during the summer of each year— in short, a world still habitable by beings analogous to those that people the earth.

This epoch marked the apogee of the human race. Thenceforward the conditions of life grew less favorable, and from century to century, from generation to generation, underwent marked change. Vegetable and animal

species, the human race itself, everything in short, became
transformed. But whereas, hitherto, these metamorphoses
had enriched, embellished and perfected life, the day had
come when decadence was to begin.

During more than a hundred thousand years it was
insensible, for the parabolic curve of life did not suddenly
fall away from its highest point. Humanity had reached
a degree of civilization, of intellectual greatness, of physical and moral well-being, of scientific, artistic and industrial perfection, incomparably beyond anything of which
we know. For several million years the central heat of the
globe had been utilized in winter for general warming purposes by towns, villages, manufactories and every variety
of industry. When this failing source of heat had finally
become exhausted, the heat of the sun had been stored
subject to the wants of the race, hydrogen had been extracted from sea-water, the energy of waterfalls, and subsequently that of the tides, had been transformed into light
and heat, and the entire planet had become the plaything
of science, which disposed at will of all its elements. The
human senses, perfected to a degree which we should now
qualify as supernatural, and those newly acquired, men-
tioned above, become with the lapse of time more highly
developed; humanity released more and more from the
empire of matter ; a new system of alimentation ; the
spirit governing the body and the gross appetites of former times forgotten ; the psychic faculties in perpetual

play, acting at a distance over the entire surface of the globe, communicating under certain conditions with even the inhabitants of Mars and Venus; apparatus which we cannot imagine replacing those optical instruments with which physical astronomy had begun its investigations; the whole world made new in its perceptions and interests; an enlightened social condition from which envy and jealousy, as well as robbery, suffering and murder had disappeared—this, indeed, was a real humanity of flesh and bone like our own, but as far above it in intellectual supremacy as we are above the simians of the tertiary epoch.

Human intelligence had so completely mastered the forces of nature that it seemed as if so glorious an era never could come to an end. The decrease in the amount of water, however, commenced to alarm even the most optimistic. The great oceans had disappeared. The crust of the earth, once so thin and mobile, had gradually increased in thickness, and, notwithstanding the internal pressure, the earth had become almost completely solidified. Oscillations of the surface were no longer possible, for it had become entirely rigid. The seas which remained were confined to the tropics. The poles were frozen. The continents of olden times, where so many other foci of civilization had shone so brilliantly, were immense deserts. Step by step humanity had migrated towards the tropical zone, still watered by streams, lakes and seas.

" RUDIMENTARY SPECIES OF CRYPTOGAMS ONLY SURVIVED."

There were no more mountains, no more condensers of snow.

As the quantity of water and rainfall diminished, and, as the springs failed and the aqueous vapor of the atmosphere grew less, vegetation had entirely changed its aspect, increasing the volume of its leaves and the length of its roots, seeking in every way to absorb the humidity necessary for life. Species which had not been able to adjust themselves to the new conditions had vanished ; the rest were transformed. Not a tree or a plant with which we are familiar was to be seen. There were no oaks, nor ashes, nor elms, nor willows, and the landscape bore no resemblance to that of today. Rudimentary species of cryptogams only survived.

Like changes had taken place in the animal kingdom. Animal forms had been greatly modified. The wild species had either disappeared or been domesticated. The scarcity of water had modified the food of herbivora as well as carnivora. The most recent species, evolved from those which preceded them, were smaller, with less fat and a larger skeleton. The number of plants had sensibly decreased. Less of the carbonic acid of the air was absorbed, and a proportionally greater quantity existed in the atmosphere. As for the human race, its metamorphosis was so absolute that it was with an astonishment bordering on incredulity that one saw in geological museums fossil specimens of men of the twentieth or one hundredth century, with great brutal teeth and coarse intestines ; it was difficult to admit that organisms so gross could really be the ancestors of intellectual man.

Though millions of years had passed, the sun still poured upon the earth almost the same quantity of heat and light. At most, the loss had not exceeded one-tenth. The only difference was that the sun appeared a little yellower and a little smaller.

The moon still revolved about the earth, but more slowly. Its distance from the earth had increased and its *apparent* diameter had diminished. At the same time the period of the earth's rotation had lengthened. This slower rotatory motion of the earth, increase in the distance of the moon, and lengthening of the lunar month, were the results of the friction of the tides, whose action resembled that of a brake. If the earth and the moon last long enough, and there are still oceans and tides, calculation would enable us to predict that the time would come when the periodic time of the earth's rotation would finally equal the lunar month, so that there would be but five and one-quarter days in the year : the earth would then always present the same side to the moon. But this would require more than 150 million years. The period of which we are speaking, ten million years, is but a fifteenth of the above ; and the time of the earth's rotation, instead of being seventy times, was only four and one-half times greater than it now is, or about 110 hours.

These long days exposed the earth to the prolonged action of the sun, but except in those regions where its rays were normal to the surface, that is to say in the equatorial zone between the two tropical circles, this exposure availed nothing; the obliquity of the ecliptic had not changed; the inclination of the axis of the earth being the same, about two degrees, and the changes in the eccentricity of the earth's orbit had produced no sensible effect upon the seasons or the climate.

The human form, food, respiration, organic functions, physical and intellectual life, ideas, opinions, religion, science, language—all had changed.   Of present man almost nothing survived.

CHAPTER IV.

THE last habitable regions of the globe were two wide valleys near the equator, the basins of dried up seas ; valleys of slight depth, for the general level was almost absolutely uniform. No mountain peaks, ravines or wild gorges, not a single wooded valley or precipice was to be seen ; the world was one vast plain, from which rivers and seas had gradually disappeared. But as the action of meteorological agents, rainfall and streams, had diminished in intensity with the loss of water, the last hollows of the sea bottom had not been entirely filled up, and shallow valleys remained, vestiges of the former structure of the globe.   In these a little ice and moisture were left, but the circulation of water in the atmosphere had ceased, and the rivers flowed in subterranean channels as in invisible veins.

As the atmosphere contained no aqueous vapor, the sky was always cloudless, and there was neither rain nor snow. The sun, less dazzling and less hot than formerly, shone with the yellowish splendor of a topaz. The color of the sky was sea-green rather than blue. The volume of the atmosphere had diminished considerably. Its oxygen and nitrogen had become in part fixed in metallic combinations, as oxides and nitrides, and its carbonic acid had slowly increased, as vegetation, deprived of water, became more and more rare and absorbed an ever decreasing amount of this gas. But the mass of the earth, owing to the constant fall of meteorites, bolides and uranolites, had increased with time; so that the atmosphere, though considerably less in volume, had retained its density and exerted nearly the same pressure.

Strangely enough, the snow and ice had diminished as the earth grew cold; the cause of this low temperature was the absence of water vapor from the atmosphere, which had decreased with the superficial area of the sea. As the water penetrated the interior of the earth and the general level became more uniform, first the depth and then the area of seas had been reduced, the invisible envelope of aqueous vapor had lost its protecting power, and the day

came when the return of the heat received from the sun
was no longer prevented, it was radiated into space as
rapidly as it was received, as if it fell upon a mirror incapable of absorbing its rays.

Such was the condition of the earth. The last representatives of the human race had survived all these physical transformations solely by virtue of its genius of inven-
tion and power of adaptation. Its last efforts had been
directed toward extracting nutritious substances from the
air, from subterranean water, and from plants, and replacing the vanished vapor of the air by buildings and roofs
of glass.

It was necessary at any cost to capture these solar rays
and to prevent their radiation into space. It was easy to
store up this heat in large quantities, for the sun shone
unobscured by any cloud and the day was long—fifty-five
hours.

For a long time the efforts of architects had been solely
directed towards this imprisonment of the sun's rays and
the prevention of their dispersion during the fifty-five
hours of the night. They had succeeded in accomplish-
ing this by an ingenius arrangement of glass roofs, super-
posed one upon the other, and by movable screens. All
combustible material had long before been exhausted ; and
even the hydrogen extracted from water was difficult to
obtain.

The mean temperature in the open air during the day-

time was not very low, not falling below –10°.* Notwithstanding the changes which the ages had wrought in
vegetable life, no species of plants could exist, even in
this equatorial zone.

As for the other latitudes, they had been totally uninhabitable for thousands of years, in spite of every effort
made to live in them. In the latitudes of Paris, Nice,
Rome, Naples, Algiers and Tunis, all protective atmospheric action had ceased, and the oblique rays of the sun
had proved insufficient to warm the soil which was frozen
to a great depth, like a veritable block of ice. The world's
population had gradually diminished from ten milliards
to nine, to eight, and then to seven, one-half the surface
of the globe being then habitable. As the habitable zone
became more and more restricted to the equator, the population had still further diminished, as had also the mean
length of human life, and the day came when only a few
hundred millions remained, scattered in groups along the
equator, and maintaining life only by the artifices of a
laborious and scientific industry.

Later still, toward the end, only two groups of a few
hundred human beings were left, occupying the last surviving centers of industry. From all the rest of the globe

---

* Many readers will regard this climate quite bearable, inasmuch, as in our own
day regions may be cited whose mean temperature is much lower, yet which are nevertheless habitable, as, for example, Verchnoiansk, whose mean annual temperature is
–19.3°. But in these regions there is a summer during which the ice melts; and if in
January the temperature falls to –60°, and even lower, in July they enjoy a temperature
of fifteen and twenty degrees above zero. But at the stage which we have now reached
in the history of the world, this mean temperature of the equatorial zone was constant,
and it was impossible for ice ever to melt again.

the human race had slowly but inexorably disappeared—dried up, exhausted, degenerated, from century to century, through the lack of an assimilable atmosphere and sufficient food. Its last remnants seemed to have lapsed back into barbarism, vegetating like the Esquimaux of the north. These two ancient centers of civilization, themselves yielding to decay, had survived only at the cost of a constant struggle between industrial genius and implacable nature.

Even here, between the tropics and the equator, the two remaining groups of human beings which still contrived to exist in face of a thousand hardships which yearly became more insupportable, did so only by subsisting, so to speak, on what their predecessors had left behind. These two ocean valleys, one of which was near the bottom of what is now the Pacific ocean, the other to the south of the present island of Ceylon, had formerly been the sites of two immense cities of glass—iron and glass having been, for a long time, the materials chiefly employed in building construction. They resembled vast winter-gardens, without upper stories, with transparent ceilings of immense height. Here were to be found the last plants, except those cultivated in the subterranean galleries leading to rivers flowing under ground.

Elsewhere the surface of the earth was a ruin, and even here only the last vestiges of a vanished greatness were to be seen.

THE SOLE SURVIVORS.

In the first of these ancient cities of glass, the sole survivors were two old men, and the grandson of one of them, Omegar, who had seen his mother and sisters die, one after the other, of consumption, and who now wandered in despair through these vast solitudes. Of these old men, one had formerly been a philosopher and had consecrated his long life to the study of the history of perishing humanity; the other was a physician who had in vain sought to save from consumption the

last inhabitants of the world. Their bodies seemed
wasted by anæmia rather than by age. They were pale
as specters, with long, white beards, and only their moral
energy sustained them yet an instant against the decree of destiny. But they could not struggle longer
against this destiny, and one day Omegar found them
stretched lifeless, side by side. From the dying hands
of one fell the last history ever written, the history
of the final transformations of humanity, written half
a century before. The second had died in his laboratory while endeavoring to keep in order the nourishment tubes, automatically regulated by machinery pro-
pelled by solar engines.

The last servants, long before developed by education from the simian race, had succumbed many years
before, as had also the great majority of the animal
species domesticated for the service of humanity.
Horses, dogs, reindeers, and certain large birds used in
aerial service, yet survived, but so entirely changed
that they bore no resemblance to their progenitors.

It was evident that the race was irrevocably
doomed. Science had disappeared with scientists, art
with artists, and the survivors lived only upon the
past. The heart knew no more hope, the spirit no
ambition. The light was in the past; the future was
an eternal night. All was over. The glories of days
gone by had forever vanished. If, in preceding cen-

turies, some traveller, wandering in these solitudes, thought he had rediscovered the sites of Paris, Rome, or the brilliant capitals which had succeeded them, he was the victim of his own imagination; for these sites had not existed for millions of years, having been swept away by the waters of the sea. Vague traditions had floated down through the ages, thanks to the printing-press and the recorders of the great events of history; but even these traditions were uncertain and often false. For, as to Paris, the annals of history contained only some references to a maritime Paris; of its existence as the capital of France for thousands of years, there was no trace nor memory. The names which to us seem immortal, Confucius, Plato, Mahomet, Alexander, Cæsar, Charlemagne, and Napoleon, had perished and were forgotten. Art had, indeed, preserved noble memories; but these memories did not extend as far back as the infancy of humanity, and reached only a few million years into the past. Omegar lingered in an ancient gallery of pictures, bequeathed by former centuries, and contemplated the great cities which had disappeared. Only one of these pictures related to what had once been Europe, and was a view of Paris, consisting of a promontory projecting into the sea, crowned by an astronomical temple and gay with helicopterons circling above the lofty towers of its terraces. Immense ships were plow-

"ALL DAY LONG HE WANDERED THROUGH THE VAST GALLERIES."

ing the sea. This classic Paris was the Paris of the one hundred and seventieth century of the Christian era, corresponding to the one hundred and fifty-seventh of the astronomical era—the Paris which existed immediately prior to the final submergence of the land. Even its name had changed; for words change like persons and things. Nearby, other pictures portrayed the great but less ancient cities which had risen in America, Australia, Asia, and afterwards upon the continents which had emerged from the ocean. And so this museum of the past recalled in succession the passing pomps of humanity down to the end.

The end! The hour had struck on the time-piece of destiny. Omegar knew the life of the world henceforth was in the past, that no future existed for it, and that the present even was vanishing like the dream of a moment. The last heir of the human race felt the overwhelming sentiment of the vanity of things. Should he wait for some inconceivable miracle to save him from his fate? Should he bury his companions, and share their tomb with them? Should he endeavor to prolong for a few days, a few weeks, a few years even, a solitary, useless and despairing existence? All day long he wandered through the vast and silent galleries, and at night abandoned himself to the drowsiness which oppressed him. All about him was dark— the darkness of the sepulchre.

A sweet dream, however, stirred his slumbering thought, and surrounded his soul with a halo of angelic brightness. Sleep brought him the illusion of life. He was no longer alone. A seductive image which he had seen more than once before, stood before him. Eyes caressing as the light of heaven, deep as the infinite, gazed upon him and attracted him. He was in a garden filled with the perfume of flowers. Birds sang in the nests amid the foliage. And in the distant landscape, framed in plants and flowers, were the vast ruins of dead cities. Then he saw a lake, on whose rippling surface two swans glided, bearing a cradle from which a new-born child stretched toward him its arms.

Never had such a ray of light illuminated his soul. So deep was his emotion that he suddenly awoke, opened his eyes, and found confronting him only the somber reality. Then a sadness more terrible even than any he had known filled his whole being. He could not find an instant of repose. He rose, went to his couch, and waited anxiously for the morning. He remembered his dream, but he did not believe in it. He felt, vaguely, that another human being existed somewhere; but his degenerate race had lost, in part, its psychic power, and perhaps, also, woman always exerts upon man an attraction more powerful than that which man exerts upon woman. When the day broke,

when the last man saw the ruins of his ancient city
standing out upon the sky of dawn, when he found
himself alone with the two last dead, he realized more
than ever his unavoidable destiny, and decided to ter-
minate at once a life so hopelessly miserable.

Going into the laboratory, he sought a bottle whose
contents were well known to him, uncorked it, and
carried it to his lips, to empty it at a draught.   But,
at the very moment the vial touched his lips, he felt
a hand upon his arm.

He turned suddenly.   There was no one in the
laboratory, and in the gallery he found only the two
dead.

CHAPTER V.

IN the ruins of the other equatorial city, occupying a
once submerged valley south of the island of Ceylon,
was a young girl, whose mother and older sister had
perished of consumption and cold, and who was now
left alone, the last surviving member of the last family of the race. A few trees, of northern species, had
been preserved under the spacious dome of glass, and
beneath their scanty foliage, holding the cold hands of
her mother who had died the night before, the young

girl sat alone, doomed to death in the very flower of her age. The night was cold. In the sky above the full moon shone like a golden torch, but its yellow rays were as cold as the silver beams of the ancient Selene. In the vast room reigned the stillness and solitude of death, broken only by the young girl's breathing, which seemed to animate the silence with the semblance of life.

She was not weeping. Her sixteen years contained more experience and knowledge than sixty years of the world's prime. She knew that she was the sole survivor of this last group of human beings, and that every happiness, every joy and every hope had vanished forever. There was no present, no future; only solitude and silence, the physical and moral impossibility of life, and soon eternal sleep. She thought of the woman of bygone days, of those who had lived the real life of humanity, of lovers, wives and mothers, but to her red and tearless eyes appeared only images of death; while beyond the walls of glass stretched a barren desert, covered by the last ice and the last snow. Now her young heart beat violently in her breast, till her slender hands could no longer compress its tumult; and now life seemed arrested in her bosom, and every respiration suspended. If for a moment she fell asleep, in her dreams she played again with her laughing and care-free sister, while her mother sung in a pure and penetrating voice the beautiful inspirations of the last poets; and she seemed to see, once more, the last fêtes of a brilliant society, as if reflected from the surface of some distant mirror. Then, on awakening, these magic memories faded into the somber reality. Alone! Alone in the world, and tomorrow death, without having known life! To struggle against this unavoidable fate was useless; the decree of destiny was without appeal, and there was nothing to do but to submit, to await the inevitable end, since without food or air organic life was impossible—or else to anticipate death and deliver oneself at once from a joyless existence and a certain doom.

" ALONE!"

She passed into the bath-room, where the warm water was still flowing, although the appliances which art had designed to supply the wants of life were no longer in working order; for the last remaining servants (descendants of ancient simian species, modified, as the human race had been, by the changing conditions of life,) had also succumbed to the insufficiency of water. She plunged into the perfumed bath, turned the key which regulated the supply of electricity derived from subterranean water-courses still unfrozen, and for a moment seemed to forget the decree of destiny in the enjoyment of this refreshing rest. Had any indiscreet spectator beheld her as, standing upon the bear-skin before the large mirror, she began to arrange the tresses of her long auburn hair, he would have detected a smile upon her lips, showing that, for an instant, she was oblivious of her dark future. Passing into another room, she approached the apparatus which furnished the food of that time, extracted from the water, air, and the plants and fruits automatically cultivated in the greenhouses.

It was still in working order, like a clock which has been wound up. For thousands of years the genius of man had been almost exclusively applied to the struggle with destiny. The last remaining water had been forced to circulate in subterranean canals, where also the solar heat had been stored. The last animals had been trained to serve these machines, and the nutritious properties of the last plants had been utilized to the utmost. Men had finally succeeded in living upon almost nothing, so far as quantity was concerned; every newly discovered form of food being completely assimilable. Cities had finally been built of glass, open to the sun, to which was conveyed every substance necessary to the synthesis of the food which replaced the products of nature. But as time passed, it became more and more difficult to obtain the necessaries of life. The mine was at last exhausted. Matter had been conquered by intelligence; but the day had come when intelligence itself was overmatched, when every worker had died at his post and the earth's storehouse had been depleted. Unwilling to abandon this desperate struggle, man had put forth every effort. But he could not prevent the earth's absorption of water, and the last resources of a science which seemed greater even than nature itself had been exhausted.

Eva returned to the body of her mother, and once more took the cold hands in her own. The psychic faculties of the race in these its latter days had acquired, as we have said, transcendent powers, and she thought for a moment to summon her mother from the tomb. It seemed to her as if she must have one more approving glance, one more counsel. A single idea took possession of her, so fascinating her that she even lost the desire to die. She saw afar the soul which should respond to her own. Every man belonging to that company of which she was the last survivor had died before her birth. Woman had outlived the sex once called strong. In the pictures upon the walls of the great library, in books, engravings and statues, she saw represented the great men of the city, but she had never seen a living man ; and still dreaming, strange and disquieting forms passed before her. She was transported into an unknown and mysterious world, into a new life, and love did not seem to be yet wholly banished from earth. During the reign of cold, all electrical communication between the two last cities left upon the earth had been interrupted. Their inhabitants could speak no more with eath other, see each other no more, nor feel each other's presence. Yet she was as well acquainted with the ocean city as if she had seen it, and when she fixed her eyes upon the great terrestrial globe suspended from the ceiling of the library, and then, closing them, concentrated all her will and psychic power upon the object of her thoughts, she acted at a distance as effectively, though in a different way, as in former days men had done when communicating with each other by electricity. She called, and felt that another heard and understood. The preceding night she had transported herself to the ancient city in which Omegar lived, and had appeared to him for an instant in a dream. That very morning she had witnessed his despairing act and by a supreme effort of the will had arrested his arm. And now, stretched in her chair beside the dead body of her mother, heavy with sleep, her solitary soul wandered in dreams above the ocean city, seeking the companionship of the only mate left upon the earth. And far away, in that ocean

By G. Rochegrosse.

" SHE FELT THAT ANOTHER HEARD AND UNDERSTOOD."

city, Omegar heard her call.   Slowly, as in a dream, he ascended the platform from which the air-ships used to take their flight.   Yielding to a mysterious influence, he obeyed the distant summons. Speeding toward the west, the electric air-ship passed above the frozen regions of the tropics, once the site of the Pacific ocean, Polynesia, Malaisia and the Sunda islands, and stopped at the landing

"YOU CALLED ME. I HAVE COME."

of the crystal palace. The young girl, startled from her dream by the traveller, who fell from the air at her feet, fled in terror to the farther end of the immense hall, lifting the heavy curtain of skin which separated it from the library. When the young man reached her side, he stopped, knelt, and took her hand in his, saying simply : " You called me. I have come." And then he added : " I have known you for a long time. I knew that you existed, I have often seen you ; you are the constant thought of my heart, but I did not dare to come."

She bade him rise, saying : " My friend, I know that we are alone in the world, and that we are about to die. A will stronger than my own compelled me to call you. It seemed as if it were the supreme desire of my mother, supreme even in death. See, she sleeps thus since yesterday. How long the night is ! "

The young man, kneeling, had taken the hand of the dead, and they both stood there beside the funeral couch, as if in prayer.

He leaned gently toward the young girl, and their heads touched. He let fall the hand of the dead.

Eva shuddered. " No," she said.

Then, suddenly, he sprang to his feet in terror ; the dead woman had revived. She had withdrawn the hand which he had taken in his own, and had opened her eyes. She made a movement, looking at them.

" I wake from a strange dream," she said, without seem-

17

"'BEHOLD, WHERE WE SHALL BE TOMORROW!'"

ing surprised at the presence of Omegar. " Behold, my children, my dream ; " and she pointed to the planet Jupiter, shining with dazzling splendor in the sky.

And as they gazed upon the star, to their astonished vision, it appeared to approach them, to grow larger, to take the place of the frozen scene about them.

Its immense seas were covered with ships. Aerial fleets cleaved the air. The shores of its seas and the mouths of its great rivers were the scenes of a prodigious activity. Brilliant cities appeared, peopled by moving multitudes. Neither the details of their habitations nor the forms of these new beings could be distinguished, but one divined that here was a humanity quite different from ours, living in the bosom of another nature, having other senses at its disposal ; and one felt also that this vast world was incomparably superior to the earth.

" Behold, where we shall be tomorrow ! " said the dying woman. " We shall find there all the human race, perfected and transformed. Jupiter has received the inheritance of the earth. Our world has accomplished its mission, and life is over here below. Farewell ! "

She stretched out her arms to them ; they bent over her pale face and pressed a long kiss upon her forehead. But they perceived that this forehead was cold as marble, in spite of this strange awakening.

The dead woman had closed her eyes, to open them no more.

CHAPTER VI.

IT is sweet to live. Love atones for every loss ; in its joys all else is forgotten. Ineffable music of the heart, thy divine melody fill the soul with an ecstasy of infinite happiness ! What illustrious historians have celebrated the heroes of the world's progress, the glories of war, the conquests of mind and of spirit ! Yet after so many centuries of labor and struggle, there remained only two palpitating hearts, the kisses of two lovers. All had perished except love ; and love, the supreme sentiment, endured, shining like an inextinguishable beacon over the immense ocean of the vanished ages.

Death ! They did not dream of it. Did they not suffice for each other ? What if the cold froze their very marrow ? Did they not possess in their hearts a warmth which defied the cold of nature ? Did not the sun still shine gloriously, and was not the final doom of the world yet far distant ? Omegar bent every energy to the maintenance of the marvellous system which had been devised for the automatic extraction by chemical processes of the nutritive principles of the air, water and plants, and in this he seemed to be successful. So in other days, after the fall of the Roman empire, the barbarians had been seen to utilize during centuries the aqueducts, baths and thermal springs, all the creations of the civilization of the Cæsars, and to draw from a vanished industry the sources of their own strength.

But one day, wonderful as it was, this system gave out. The subterranean waters themselves ceased to flow. The soil was frozen to a great depth. The rays of the sun still warmed the air within the glass-covered dwellings, but no plant could live longer ; the supply of water was exhausted.

The combined efforts of science and industry were impotent to give to the atmosphere the nutritive qualities possessed by those of other worlds, and the human organism constantly clamored for the regenerating principles which, as we have seen, had been derived from the air, water and plants. These sources were now exhausted.

This last human pair struggled against these insur-
mountable obstacles, and recognized the uselessness of
farther contest, yet they were not resigned to death. Before knowing each other they had awaited it fearlessly.
Now each wished to defend the other, the beloved one,
against pitiless destiny. The very idea of seeing Omegar
lying inanimate beside her, filled Eva with such anguish
that she could not bear the thought. And he, too, vainly
longed to carry away his well beloved from a world
doomed to decay, to fly with her to that brilliant Jupiter
which awaited them, and not to abandon to the earth the
body he adored.

He thought that, perhaps, there still existed, somewhere
upon the earth, a spot which had retained a little of that
life-giving water without which existence was impossible ;
and, although already they were both almost without
strength, he formed the supreme resolution of setting out
to seek for it. The electric aeronef was still in working
order. Forsaking the city which was now only a tomb,
the two last survivors of a vanished humanity abandoned
these inhospitable regions and set out to seek some unknown oasis.

The ancient kingdoms of the world passed under their
feet. They saw the remains of great cities, made illustrious by the splendors of civilization, lying in ruins
along the equator. The silence of death covered them
all. Omegar recognized the ancient city which he had

recently left, but he knew that there, also the supreme source of life was lacking, and they did not stop. They traversed thus, in their solitary air-ship, the regions which had witnessed the last stages of the life of human-ity; but death, and silence, and the frozen desert was everywhere. No more fields, no more vegetation; the watercourses were visible as on a map, and it was evi-dent that along their banks life had been prolonged; but they were now dried up forever. And when, at times, some motionless lake was distinguished in the lower level, it was like a lake of stone; for even at the equator the sun was powerless to melt the eternal ice. A kind of bear, with long fur, was still to be seen wandering over the frozen earth, seeking in the crevices of the rocks its scanty vegetable food. From time to time, also, they descried a kind of penguin and sea-cows walking upon the ice, and large, gray polar birds in awkward flight, or alighting mournfully.

Nowhere was the sought-for oasis found. The earth was indeed dead.

Night came. Not a cloud obscured the sky. A warmer current from the south had carried them over what was formerly Africa, now a frozen waste. The mechanism of the aeronef had ceased to work. Ex-hausted by cold rather than by hunger, they threw themselves upon the bear-skins in the bottom of the car.

By O. Guillonnet.

"A WHITE SHADOW STOPPED BEFORE THEIR ASTONISHED EYES."

Perceiving a ruin, they alighted. It was an immense quadrangular base, revealing traces of an enormous stone stairway. It was still possible to recognize one of the ancient Egyptian pyramids which, in the middle of the desert, survived the civilization which it represented. With all Egypt, Nubia and Abyssinia, it had sunk below the level of the sea, and had afterwards emerged into the light and been restored in the heart of a new capital by a new civilization, more brilliant than that of Thebes and of Memphis, and finally had been again abandoned to the desert. It was the only remaining monument of the earlier life of humanity, and owed its stability to its geometric form.

"Let us rest here," said Eva, "since we are doomed to die. Who, indeed, has escaped death? Let me die in peace in your arms."

They sought a corner of the ruin and sat down beside each other, face to face with the silent desert. The young girl cowered upon the ground, pressing her husband in her arms, still striving with all her might against the penetrating cold. He drew her to his heart, and warmed her with his kisses.

"I love you, and I am dying," she said. "But, no, we will not die. See that star, which calls us!"

At the same moment they heard behind them a slight noise, issuing from the ancient tomb of Cheops, a noise like that the wind makes in the leaves. Shuddering, they turned, together, in the direction whence the sound came. A white shadow, which seemed to be self-luminous, for the night was already dark and there was no moon, glided rather than walked toward them, and stopped before their astonished eyes.

" Fear nothing," it said. " I come to seek you. No, you shall not die. No one has ever died. Time flows into eternity ; eternity remains.

" I was Cheops, King of Egypt, and I reigned over this country in the early days of the world. As a slave, I have since expiated my crimes in many existences, and when at length my soul deserved immortality I lived upon Neptune, Ganymede, Rhea, Titan, Saturn, Mars, and other worlds as yet unknown to you. Jupiter is now my home. In the days of humanity's greatness, Jupiter was not habitable for intelligent beings. It was passing through the necessary stages of preparation. Now this immense world is the heir to all human achievement. Worlds succeed each other in time as in space. All is eternal, and merges into the divine. Confide in me, and follow me."

And as the old Pharaoh was still speaking, they felt a delicious fluid penetrate their souls, as sometimes the ear is filled with an exquisite melody. A sense of calm and transcendent happiness flowed in their veins. Never, in any dream, in any ecstasy, had they ever experienced such joy.

Eva pressed Omegar in her arms. " I love you," she

By O. Guillonnet.

" THE SPECTRE ROSE INTO SPACE."

repeated. Her voice was only a breath. He touched his
lips to her already cold mouth, and heard them murmur :
" How I could have loved ! "

Jupiter was shining majestically above them, and in the
glorious light of his rays their sight grew dim and their
eyes gently closed.

The spectre rose into space and vanished. And one to
whom it is given to see, not with the bodily eyes, which
perceive only material vibrations, but with the eyes of the
soul, which perceive psychical vibrations, might have seen
two small flames shining side by side, united by a common attraction, and rising, together with the phantom,
into the heavens.

EPILOGUE.

"And the angel lifted up his hand to heaven and sware by Him that liveth forever and ever that there should be time no longer."—Rev. x., 6.

Φ

THE earth was dead. The other planets also had died one after the other. The sun was extinguished. But the stars still shone; there were still suns and worlds.

In the measureless duration of eternity, time, an essentially relative conception, is determined by each world, and even in each world this conception is dependent upon the consciousness of the individual. Each world measures its own duration. The year of the earth is not that of Neptune. The latter is 164 times the former, and yet is not longer relatively to the absolute. There is no common measure between time and eternity. In empty space there is no time, no years, no centuries; only the possibility of a measurement of time which becomes real the moment a revolving world appears. Without some periodic motion no conception whatever of time is possible.

The earth no longer existed, nor her celestial companion, the little isle of Mars, nor the beautiful sphere of Venus, nor the colossal world of Jupiter, nor the strange universe of Saturn, which had lost its rings, nor the slow-moving Uranus and Neptune—not even the glorious sun, in whose fecundating heat these mansions of the heavens had basked for so many centuries. The sun was a dark ball, the planets also ; and still this invisible system sped on in the glacial cold of starry space. So far as life is concerned, all these worlds were dead, did not exist. They survived their past history like the ruins of the dead cities of Assyria which the archæologist uncovers in the desert, moving on their way in darkness through the invisible and the unknown.

No genius, no magician could recall the vanished past, when the earth floated bathed in light, with its broad green fields waking to the morning sun, its rivers winding like long serpents through the verdant meadows, its woods alive with the songs of birds, its forests filled with deep and mysterious shadows, its seas heaving with the tides or roaring in the tempest, its mountain slopes furrowed with rushing streams and cascades, its gardens enameled with flowers, its nests of birds and cradles of children, and its toiling population, whose activity had transformed it and who lived so joyously a life perpetuated by the delights of an endless love. All this happiness seemed eternal. What has become of those mornings and evenings, of those flowers and those lovers, of that light and perfume, of those harmonies and joys, of those beauties and dreams? All is dead, has disappeared in the darkness of night.

The world dead, all the planets dead, the sun extinguished. The solar system annihilated, time itself suspended.

Time lapses into eternity. But eternity remains, and time is born again.

Before the existence of the earth, throughout an eternity, suns and worlds existed, peopled with beings like ourselves. Millions of years before the earth was, they were. The past of the universe has been as brilliant as the present, the future will be as the past, the present is of no importance.

In examining the past history of the earth, we might go back to a time when our planet shone in space, a veritable sun, appearing as Jupiter and Saturn do now, shrouded in a dense atmosphere charged with warm vapors ; and we might follow all its transformations down to the period of man. We have seen that when its heat was entirely dissipated, its waters absorbed, the aqueous vapor of its atmosphere gone, and this atmosphere itself more or less absorbed, our planet must have presented the appearance of those great lunar deserts seen through the telescope (with certain differences due to the action of causes peculiar to the earth), with its final geographical configurations, its dried-up shores and water-courses, a planetary corpse, a dead and frozen world. It still bears, however, within its bosom an unexpended energy—that of its motion of translation about the sun, an energy which, transformed into heat by the sudden destruction of its motion, would suffice to melt it and to reduce it, in part, to a state of vapor, thus inaugurating a new epoch ; but for an instant only, for, if this motion of translation were destroyed, the earth would fall into the sun and its independent existence would come to an end. If suddenly arrested it would move in a straight line toward the sun, with an increasing velocity, and reach the sun in sixty-five days ; were its motion gradually arrested, it would move in a spiral, to be swallowed up, at last, in the central luminary.

The entire history of terrestrial life is before our eyes. It has its commencement and its end ; and its duration, however many the centuries which compose it, is preceded and followed by eternity—is, indeed, but a single instant lost in eternity.

For a long time after the earth had ceased to be the abode of life, the colossal worlds of Jupiter and Saturn, passing more slowly from their solar to their planetary stage, reigned in their turn among the planets, with the splendor of a vitality incomparably superior to that of our earth. But they, also, waxed old and descended into the night of the tomb.

X

Had the earth, like Jupiter, for example, retained long enough the elements of life, death would have come only with the extinction of the sun. But the length of the life of a world is proportional to its size and its elements of vitality.

The solar heat is due to two principal causes—the condensation of the original nebula, and the fall of meteorites. According to the best established calculations of thermodynamics, the former has produced a quantity of heat eighteen million times greater than that which the sun radiates yearly, supposing the original nebula was cold, which there is no reason to believe was the case. It is, therefore, certain that the solar temperature produced by this condensation far exceeded the above. If condensation continues, the radiation of heat may go on for centuries without loss.

The heat emitted every second is equal to that which would result from the combustion of eleven quadrillions six hundred thousand milliards of tons of coal burning at once! The earth intercepts only one five hundredth millionth part of the radiant heat, and this one five hundredth millionth suffices to maintain all terrestrial life. Of sixty-seven millions of light and heat rays which the sun radiates into space, only one is received and utilized by the planets.

Well! to maintain this source of heat it is only necessary that the rate of condensation should be such that the sun's diameter should decrease seventy-seven meters a year, or one kilo-meter in thirteen years. This con-traction is so gradual that it would be wholly imperceptible. Nine thousand five hundred years would be required to re-duce the diameter by one single second of arc. Even if the sun be actually in a gaseous state, its temperature, so

far from growing less, or even remaining stationary, would increase by the very fact of contraction; for if on the one hand the temperature of a gaseous body falls when it condenses, on the other hand the heat generated by contraction is more than sufficient to prevent a fall in temperature, and the amount of heat increases until a liquid state is reached. The sun seems to have reached this stage.

The condensation of the sun, whose density is only one-fourth that of the earth, may thus of itself maintain for centuries, at least for ten million years, the light and heat of this brilliant star. But we have just spoken of a second source of heat : the fall of meteorites. One hundred and forty-six million meteorites fall upon the earth yearly. A vastly greater number fall into the sun, because of its greater attraction. If their mass equals about the one hundredth part of the mass of the earth, their fall would suffice to maintain the temperature,—not by their combustion, for if the sun itself was being consumed it would not have lasted more than six thousand years, but by the sudden transformation of the energy of motion into heat, the velocity of impact being 650,000 meters per second, so great is the solar attraction.

If the earth should fall into the sun, it would make good for ninety-five years the actual loss of solar energy; Venus would make good this loss for eighty-four years; Mercury for seven; Mars for thirteen; Jupiter for 32,254; Saturn for 9652; Uranus for 1610; and Neptune for 1890 years. That is to say, the fall of all the planets into the sun would produce heat enough to maintain the present rate of expenditure for about 46,000 years.

It is therefore certain that the fall of meteors greatly lengthens the life of the sun. One thirty-third mill-

ionth of the solar mass added each year would com-
pensate for the loss, and half of this would be sufficient if we admit that condensation shares equally with
the fall of meteorites in the maintenance of solar heat;
centuries would have to pass before any acceleration
of the planets' velocities would be apparent.

Owing to these two causes alone we may, therefore,
admit a future for the sun of at least twenty million years;
and this period cannot but be increased by other unknown
causes, to say nothing of an encounter with a swarm of
meteorites.

The sun therefore was the last living member of the system; the last animated by the warmth of life.

But the sun also went out.   After having so long poured
upon his celestial children his vivifying beams, the black
spots upon his surface increased in number and in extent,
his brilliant photosphere grew dull, and his hitherto dazzling surface became congealed.   An enormous red ball
took the place of the dazzling center of the vanished worlds.

For a long time this enormous star maintained a high
surface temperature, and a sort of phosphorescent atmosphere; its virgin soil, illumined by the light of the stars
and by the electric influences which formed a kind of atmosphere, gave birth to a marvelous flora, to an unknown
fauna, to beings differing absolutely in organization from
those who had succeeded each other upon the worlds of its
system.

But for the sun also the end came, and the hour sounded on the timepiece of destiny when the whole solar system was stricken from the book of life. And one after another the stars, each one of which is a sun, a solar system, shared the same fate; yet the universe continued to exist as it does today.

Ψ

The science of mathematics tells us: "The solar system does not appear to possess at present more than the one four hundred and fifty-fourth part of the transformable energy which it had in the nebulous state. Although this remainder constitutes a fund whose magnitude confounds our imagination, it will also some day be exhausted. Later, the transformation will be complete for the entire universe, resulting in a general equilibrium of temperature and pressure.

" Energy will not then be susceptible of transformation. This does not mean annihilation, a word without meaning, nor does it mean the absence of motion, properly speaking, since the same sum of energy will always exist in the form of atomic motion, but the absence of all sensible motion, of all differentiation, the absolute uniformity of conditions, that is to say, absolute death."

Such is the present statement of the science of mathematics.

Experiment and observation prove that on the one hand the quantity of matter, and on the other hand the quantity of energy also, remains constant, whatever the change in form or in position ; but they also show that the universe tends to a state of equilibrium, a condition in which its heat will be uniformly distributed.

The heat of the sun and of all the stars seems to be due to the transformation of their initial energy of motion, to molecular impacts ; the heat thus generated is being constantly radiated into space, and this radiation will go on until every sun is cooled down to the temperature of space itself.

If we admit that the sciences of today, mechanics, physics and mathematics, are trustworthy, and that the laws which now control the operations of nature and of reason are permanent, this must be the fate of the universe.

Far from being eternal, the earth on which we live has had a beginning. In eternity a hundred million years, a thousand million years or centuries, are as a day. There is an eternity behind us and before us, and all apparent duration is but a point. A scientific investigation of nature and acquaintance with its laws raises, therefore, the question already raised by the theologians, whether Plato, Zoroaster, Saint Augustine, Saint Thomas Aquinas, or some young seminarist who has just taken orders : " What was God doing before the creation of the universe, and

what will he do after its end?" Or, under a less anthro-
morphic form, since God is unknowable : " What was the
condition of the universe prior to the present order of
things, and what will it be after this order has passed
away ? "

Note that the question is the same, whether we admit a
personal God, reasoning and acting toward a definite end,
or, whether we deny the existence of any spiritual being,
and admit only the existence of indestructible atoms and
forces representing an invariable sum of energy.

In the first case, why should God, an eternal and
uncreated power, remain inactive ? Or, having remained
inactive, satisfied with the absolute infinity of his nature which nothing could augment, why did he change
this state and create matter and force ?

The theologian may reply : " Because it was his good
pleasure. " But philosophy is not satisfied with this
change in the divine purpose. In the second case, since
the origin of the present condition of things only dates
back a certain time, and since there can be no effect
without a cause, we have the right to ask what was the
condition of things anterior to the formation of the
present universe.

Although energy is indestructible, we certainly cannot
deny the tendency toward its universal dissipation, and
this must lead to absolute repose and death, for the conclusions of mathematics are irresistible.

Nevertheless, we do not concede this.

Why?

Because the universe is not a definite quantity.

Ω

It is impossible to conceive of a limit to the extension of matter. Limitless space, the inexhaustible source of the transformation of potential energy into visible motion, and thence into heat and other forces, confronts us, and not a simple, finished piece of mechanism, running like a clock and stopping forever.

The future of the universe is its past. If the universe were to have had an end, this end would have been reached long ago, and we should not be here to study this problem.

It is because our conceptions are finite, that things have a beginning and an end. We cannot conceive of an absolutely endless series of transformations, either in the future or in the past, nor that an equally endless series of material combinations, of planets, suns, sun-systems, milky ways, stellar universes, can succeed each other. Nevertheless, the heavens are there to show us the infinite. Nor can we comprehend any better the infinity of space or of time ; yet it is impossible for us to conceive of a limit to either, for our thought overleaps the limit, and is

impotent to conceive of bounds beyond which there is no
space nor time. One may travel forever, in any direction, without reaching a boundary, and as soon as anyone
affirms that at a certain moment duration ceases, we refuse
our assent ; for we cannot confound time with the human
measures of it.

These measures are relative and arbitrary ; but time
itself exists, like space, independently of them. Suppress
everything, space and time would still remain ; that is to
say, space which material things may occupy, and the possibility of the succession of events. If this were not so,
neither space nor time would be really measurable, not
even in thought, since thought would not exist. But it is
impossible for the mind even to suppress either the one or
the other. Strictly speaking, it is neither space nor time
that we are speaking of, but infinity and eternity, relative to which every measure, however great, is but a
point.

We do not comprehend or conceive of infinite space or
time, because we are incapable of it. But this incapacity
does not invalidate the existence of the absolute. In confessing that we do not comprehend infinity, we feel it
about us, and that space, as bounded by a wall or any
barrier whatever, is in itself an absurd idea. And we are
equally incapable of denying the possibility of the existence, at some instant of time, of a system of worlds whose
motions would measure time without creating it. Do our

clocks create time ? No, they do but measure it. In the presence of the absolute, our measures of both time and space vanish ; but the absolute remains.

We live, then, in the infinite, without doubting it for an instant. The hand which holds this pen is composed of eternal and indestructible elements, and the atoms which constituted it existed in the solar nebula whence our planet came, and will exist forever. Your lungs breathe, your brains think, with matter and forces which acted millions of years ago and will act endlessly. And the little globule which we inhabit floats, not at the center of a limited universe, but in the depth of infinity, as truly as does the most distant star which the telescope can discover.

The best definition of the universe ever given, to which there was nothing to add, is Pascal's, " A sphere whose center is everywhere and circumference nowhere."

It is this infinity which assures the eternity of the universe.

Stars, systems, myriads, milliards, universes succeed each other without end in every direction.

We do not live near a center which does not exist, and the earth, like the farthest star, lies in the fathomless infinite.

No bounds to space. Fly in thought in any direction with any velocity for months, years, centuries, forever, we shall meet with no limit, approach no boundary, we shall always remain in the vestibule of the infinite before us.

No bounds to time. Live in imagination through future ages, add centuries to centuries, epoch to epoch, we shall never attain the end, we shall always remain in the vestibule of the eternity which opens before us.

In our little sphere of terrestrial observation we see that, through all the transformations of matter and motion, the same quantity of each remains, though under new forms. Living beings afford a perpetual illustration of this : they are born, they grow by appropriating substances from the world without, and when they die they break up and restore to nature the elements of which they are composed. But by a law whose action never ceases other bodies are constituted from these same elements. Every star may be likened to an organized being, even as regards its internal heat. A body is alive so long as respiration and the circulation of the blood makes it possible for the various organs to perform their functions. When equilibrium and repose are reached, death follows ; but after death all the substances of which the body was formed are wrought into other beings. Dissolution is the prelude to recreation. Analogy leads us to believe that the same is true of the cosmos. Nothing can be destroyed.

There is an incommensurable Power, which we are obliged to recognize as limitless in space and without be-

ginning or end in time, and this Power is that which persists through all the changes in those sensible appearances under which the universe presents itself to us.

For this reason there will always be suns and worlds, not like ours, but still suns and worlds succeeding each other through all eternity.

And for us this visible universe can only be the changing *appearance* of the absolute and eternal *reality.*

A

It is in virtue of this transcendent law that, long after the death of the earth, of the giant planets and the central luminary, while our old and darkened sun was still speeding through boundless space, with its dead worlds on which terrestrial and planetary life had once engaged in the futile struggle for daily existence, another extinct sun, issuing from the depths of infinity, collided obliquely with it and brought it to rest!

Then in the vast night of space, from the shock of these two mighty bodies was suddenly kindled a stupendous conflagration, and an immense gaseous nebula was formed, which trembled for an instant like a flaring flame, and then sped on into regions unknown. Its temperature was several million degrees. All which here below had been earth, water, air, minerals, plants, atoms; all which had constituted man, his flesh, his palpitating

heart, his flashing eye, his armed hand, his thinking
brain, his entrancing beauty ; the victor and the van-
quished, the executioner and his victim, and those inferior souls still wearing the fetters of matter,—all were
changed into fire. And so with the worlds of Mars,
Venus, Jupiter, Saturn, and the rest. It was the resurrection of visible nature. But those superior souls which
had acquired immortality continued to live forever in
the hierarchy of the invisible psychic universe. The
conscious existence of mankind had attained an ideal
state. Mankind had passed by transmigration through
the worlds to a new life with God, and freed from the
burdens of matter, soared with an endless progress in
eternal light.

The immense gaseous nebula, which absorbed all
former worlds, thus transformed into vapor, began to turn
upon itself. And in the zones of condensation of this
primordial star-mist, new worlds were born, as heretofore
the earth was.

So another universe began, whose genesis some future
Moses and Laplace would tell, a new creation, extra-
terrestrial, superhuman, inexhaustible, resembling neither
the earth nor Mars, nor Saturn, nor the sun.

And new humanities arose, new civilizations, new vanities, another Babylon, another Thebes, another Athens,
another Rome, another Paris, new palaces, temples, glories
and loves. And all these things possessed nothing of

the earth, whose very memory had passed away like a shadow.

And these universes passed away in their turn. But infinite space remained, peopled with worlds, and stars, and souls, and suns; and time went on forever.

For there can be neither end nor beginning.